PRAISE FOR
SERGIO CHEJFEC

"*The Incompletes* is a masterfully nested narrative where writing—its presence on the page, its course through time, its prismatic dispersion of meaning—is the true protagonist. Heather Cleary's flawless translation adds yet another layer to this extraordinary palimpsest of a novel."
—Hernan Diaz

"*The Incompletes* is, simply put, Chejfec's best book, a 'thriller' in a way, although the thing that gets me is how it's also an inside-out *Madame Bovary*."
—Javier Molea, McNally Jackson

"On first reading Chejfec, we recall many admired authors, but at a later moment—a more solid and lasting one—we realize that he resembles no one, and that he has chosen an unusual and quite distinctive path, one that reveals itself slowly because of the demanding and very personal searches the author himself carries out in his narrative."
—Enrique Vila-Matas

"It is hard to think of another contemporary writer who, marrying true intellect with simple description of a space, simultaneously covers so little and so much ground."
—*Times Literary Supplement*

"If genius can be defined by the measure of depth of an artist's perception into human experience, then Chejfec is a genius."
—*Coffin Factory*

Other works by Sergio Chejfec

Baroni: A Journey
The Dark
My Two Worlds
The Planets

THE

INCOMPLETES

SERGIO CHEJFEC

Translated from the Spanish
by Heather Cleary

OPEN LETTER
LITERARY TRANSLATIONS FROM THE UNIVERSITY OF ROCHESTER

The citation from *A Complicated Mammal* by Joaquín O. Giannuzzi is taken from Richard Gwyn's 2012 translation, published by CB Editions.

Library of Congress Cataloging-in-Publication Data: Available.
ISBN-13: 978-1-948830-03-4 / ISBN-10: 1-948830-03-5

This project is supported in part by the New York State Council on the Arts with the support of Governor Andrew M. Cuomo and the New York State Legislature.

Printed on acid-free paper in the United States of America.

Text set in Fournier, a typeface designed by Pierre Simon Fournier (1712–1768), a French punch-cutter, typefounder, and typographic theoretician.

Design by Anthony Blake

Open Letter is the University of Rochester's nonprofit, literary translation press: Dewey Hall 1-219, Box 278968, Rochester, NY 14627

www.openletterbooks.org

THE
INCOMPLETES

Now I am going to tell the story of something that happened one night, years ago, and the events of the morning and afternoon that followed. Ending a day the same as any other—nightfall, exhaustion, silence, solitude—during those final domestic acts one performs with resignation and mounting fear, wondering if that night will be the last, if the world will vanish while we sleep, or if our soul will wake to find itself forever separated from its body—from that night's protracted beginning until the moment I nodded off, my thoughts turned insistently to a friend I hadn't seen, I haven't seen, in years. When we were young, a time nearly forgotten and from which decades separate us, he decided to leave his country and survive in the world like a wandering planet, to steep himself in the languages he would pick up along the way and, among other things, to take on a vague international luster (always bearing the ambiguous yoke, both brutal and enviable, barely visible yet indelible, of being an Argentinian in flight).

I should say "I haven't forgotten," rather than invoke memory. Of the morning when he left, I haven't forgotten the empty port, a little blue stall with a white roof, trees scattered as if by chance across the surrounding area, and, above all, the piers and the repetitive backdrop of nautical equipment (cranes, jetties, tracks, and moorings) at the ready, though they seemed gratuitous in the absence of more people or other ships. I got there early and waited. (It seems to me now that time was more complex in my youth: I was waiting for someone who was about to leave, as if waiting had asserted itself in advance as a cause—this was why the days passed so slowly; maddeningly drawn out, they sometimes even seemed to grind to a halt and the whole idea of reality, along with the idea of nature concealed within it, presented itself as distressingly multiple and unpredictable.) The pier was just a damp promenade; drops of dew fell from the roof of the little stall, and the slowly dissolving night still hid the water's surface like an immense, uninhabited depression. The wait seemed to suit the occasion—even if you understood time as an unstoppable thing set in motion, its languor, or rather its apathy, was still surprising: the morning's lack of urgency to arrive.

A long time passed like that, I think. Distant lights slowed their flickering in the sky; just as they threatened to go out altogether, I saw a car approach slowly and what might be described as shakily, probably because of the cobblestones. It was the taxi that had brought Felix. The car rolled forward for what I considered a theatrically long time. And then nothing happened. Felix remained inside for no reason at all, like a stage actor delaying his entrance, though I had no way of knowing that. After a while he opened the door and started removing his luggage. I thought he'd never finish—at first glance, it seemed impossible that the suitcases and packages piled beside the car could have fit inside. (It reminded me of those comedic scenes of trunks or vans spouting endless streams of objects.) Then the taxi drove off and Felix was left standing in the middle of the street, flanked by two sizeable heaps. Suddenly alone, he had trouble getting his bearings. I could tell he was paralyzed, probably completely overwhelmed to find himself out in the open and even more so by the task ahead of him; I don't mean just the ordeal of moving his luggage, but rather the act of recognizing it for the first time as a surrogate of himself: silent and necessary additions, an extension of his body bound to follow him for a long time to come . . . That was when he saw me, almost hidden in the half-light of dawn, and I in turn saw his surprise at my being there early.

The characteristic scent of Buenos Aires, a mix of aquatic plants and the local soil, which—as many have told me and I've also read—still filters through the streets on the breeze, was an incipient aroma slowly rising off the river to form waves of disparate and paradoxically incomplete smells that morning, probably due to the hour. Here, the memory skips to the next scene: we take a few indecisive steps toward a warehouse's loading dock, where—with nothing better to do as we wait for the still-empty pier to spring into action and fill with people—we begin to talk. I've forgotten the essential parts of that conversation; I retain most vividly the image of a few very large, very yellow kernels of corn that had fallen between the paving stones, at which I stared intently the entire time. They stood out as a glimmer of life protected deep in the rock, in crevices that pigeons would later try to rob of their prize, rarely with any success.

The fact is, every so often I receive a few invariably brief lines from Felix in which he casually summarizes the recent events of his life. I don't know whether to call it coincidence, a premonition, or some kind of message, but just hours after I remembered him, after his presence asserted itself and no other thought could eclipse the ideas associated with him, that same presence spontaneously materialized the next morning, translated into a simple postcard sent by Felix—an act that was surely less eloquent than the meaning it took on through the coincidence. A day like any other: nothing had happened to make Felix occupy my thoughts the way he did for much of that night and the following day, when I finally sat to jot down a few notes about it as a way to welcome a mental visit that at once conceals and consolidates distance.

A long time often goes by without Felix sending word from somewhere he has moved or is passing through. He typically uses cheap or free postcards, or sheets of hotel stationery. Before I read or receive them, and probably before Felix even writes them, these messages are already old-fashioned, archaic; they have the quality of obsolete correspondence. I'm not talking about our friendship, but rather the paper itself, that stiff material faded by the passage of time. On occasion it has occurred to me to think about how long a postcard would need to sit in one of those stands to look like that, or about those envelopes embellished with the kind of flourishes you see on school diplomas, all distinctly sepia. Felix's handwriting is tentative, or maybe I should say nervous or emotional; it suggests an inhibition whose underlying motives only he can reveal. He announces some "new battlefield," as he calls it, that is, a change of activity and place. Leaving the country was an attempt to free himself from the bonds of nationality in favor of other, more fluid ones that would protect him, illusorily, from the decisions of any single State and from the emotional effects of what happened there. As a citizen of the world—"What does that mean, anyway?" he asked in one of his early notes, more frequent after he first left—like any good citizen of the world, Felix tempers his defining characteristics according to a series of ever-changing conventions. It's not that he is conventional; he simply realized that the anonymity he sought, in order to be such, should resemble uniformity—and, by extension, predictability.

He even sent me a postcard once from Buenos Aires: a partial view of its taciturn bus terminal with a police car crossing the avenue in the foreground. Several hundred meters behind the building, the background offers a glimpse of a monument blurred by the distance and, presumably, by the city's noxious air; to its right, two rows of buses all painted the same dark color seem to be paying it some incrutable military tribute. The image on the postcard, which appeared to have been captured in a rush, managed to seem less like a photograph than like a glance cast by one of the thousands of people who pass through there every day, not seeing anything in particular. It was as if Felix were saying, beyond the content of his terse, hand-written note, "Here I am, so immersed in this movement, the confusion and the daily grind, that I've grabbed an artless postcard that says exactly the opposite of what you would expect and dissolves into a conventional panorama."

One could, in fact, picture someone reaching Buenos Aires after days at the mercy of the continent's endless highways, and imagine this person feeling relieved or even happy rather than dejected, despite the gloomy scenery offered by that part of the city, to have reached their journey's end. After getting off the bus, the passenger immediately forgets the trip (a recent, but curiously faded, ordeal); nonetheless, by some strange mechanism he is able to recall the roads, the passing days, and the gradual transformations along the route; he can also imagine, without error, how much of what he has seen remains the same and probably will forever. For example, that the eatery next to the gas station where they stopped one morning is still there, and so is the bathroom where he let water run for a long time over his hands. The traveler imagines all these elements (bathroom, sink, eatery, highway) with their blind, mismatched routines as the nuclei or eternal wellsprings of experiences, given over to their own phenomenon: having shown a fleeting relevance, they might continue on like that indefinitely, at the disposal of whoever might pass through and wish to make the same use of them. In the midst of this contradiction between the fresh memory of his journey and the impersonal existence of the landscape that the recently arrived realizes that the gloomy postcard panorama that is morning in Buenos Aires is the only event of any value he can cling to; it may be a sad and miserly spectacle but, ultimately it is proof of what that arrival represents.

Another time, a postcard with the words "Plaza Catalunya" printed on it arrived from Barcelona. I looked at the image and couldn't understand it at first. Much of its surface was taken up by the awning, printed in different colors and languages, of what appeared to be a tourist information center. The sign was too big; it took up the entire width of the postcard and had the effect of making the office's glass doors, at the end of a flight of stairs leading down from street level, look even smaller. I thought of shiny plastic miniatures fabricated for the sole purpose of revealing the existence of a baroque and artificial nature that typically remains hidden but sometimes, only sometimes, is revealed. This confusing ornamentation, which the sign's vibrant colors were meant to offset, provoked an even greater sense of disorientation: it felt as if you were standing at the entrance to an underground walkway that offered only the cold comfort of even illumination in contrast to the sordid darkness underground. Above the tourist information center was the plaza, while below and to its sides were the unfamiliar world of things buried, and, a few hundred meters away, the deep waters of the drowsy, boundless sea.

A section of the plaza appeared in a thin horizontal strip at the top of the postcard; leaning over the handrail above the hollow carved out by the stairs, a few people were killing time in the big city. Anonymous shadows, irregular silhouettes, different clothes. They looked like cutouts, mannequins dressed and arranged to represent, each with its unique outline, the contours of a group. I looked more closely and could distinguish two buses crossing the avenue in the background. Some kind of plastic monolith topped with a pinwheel had been erected on the sidewalk; another indication of the tourist information center beneath, I thought, based on the colors. For a moment, I imagined those people leaning on the counter inside; then I mentally transposed the office onto the surface of the plaza, like a full-scale blueprint placed in a larger setting. In that case, the people at the counter would either be employees or curious tourists waiting for information in the designated spot, but in the wrong way, without anyone around them noticing the error or any means of putting their space, as it were, back in its place. It seemed clear to me that by sending that postcard, Felix was trying to hide behind the mask of the hurried or distracted individual who chooses a point crossed by people of different origins in order to leave a trace of his movement far from there (that is, in the postcard I would receive at a great distance); it also seemed to me that this simple postcard, just like the event itself, that is, his footsteps going up or down those stairs, was destined to be fleeting and, above all, forgotten. Still, one could think of those figures with their backs turned as the theatrical epicenter of the city, the personification (though they lacked faces or identities) of an urban brain without which everything would come apart. It didn't matter if the silhouettes were cut-outs made of cardboard or wood—in fact, the more artificial they were, the better.

Felix went into a shop where they sold lottery tickets, stood transfixed for a moment by the packs of cigarettes, loose tobacco, pens, and lighters, then sent the postcard. When he stepped back into the street he wondered what he'd been doing; cities inhabited by indistinguishable bodies confused him. His attempt to return to his hotel took him on a detour that cost him half a day; during that time, he walked without thinking about anything, or was overcome by the lethargy produced by wide open or densely populated spaces. A life on loan, pawned life, fabricated life—Felix thought of several other options. The streets looked to him like an ostentatious theatrical backdrop: thousands of people synchronized in their movements and alert to Felix and his trajectory, staging a representation, probably of themselves, as they saturated the landscape and filled the city to the point of overflowing. This act was, however, useless: there was nothing unique in it. He was still at the first hotel he'd checked in to when he arrived; he had seen an understated sign on the front of a building, too far from the door to clearly belong with it, which read, "Samich Guesthouse." He'd made himself go inside, though his first thought was that they wouldn't have a room for him. With his first steps, he left the noise of the street behind; Felix sensed he was somewhere else, an abandoned enclosure in the epicenter of the city or a place lost on the map. The silence, the cavern's thrum, the cool shade of tall buildings. Further in, he found a sign on the dark wall like the one he'd seen from the street, but smaller and so timeworn it was hard to read; set apart from that (as solitary as a light switch) he saw an old doorbell with a loose button he immediately started fiddling with, in vain. He began to think about that house, but the ideas were incomplete and never fully coalesced, most likely due to his impatience. Just as he was about to give up and leave, he heard voices that made him think someone was coming to let him in.

When he stepped into the reception area he felt as if he'd been transported to another place, one completely different from everything he knew, where small things reigned. Had it not been for the Dominican owner and her improvements to the space—the walls covered with simple, brightly colored decorations and Caribbean hammocks hung too close together like tattered scraps of fabric—Felix would have made a run for it to save himself from the unease that saturated the shadows, and the space in general. The owner and her teenage daughter (who was Cuban and, he would discover moments later, spoke as such) stood on the other side of the counter. This unusual Antillean combination intrigued Felix; he began imagining explanations and possible routes, clandestine trips, bitter disputes, name changes, escapes, and adoptions. At one point, a door slammed and the sound of a radio, which had been clear before, became something like a vibration emanating from the walls. Behind the women were shelves littered with objects that at first glance appeared useless and forgotten, as if their principal virtue was simply remaining where they were with a defiant attitude toward the luck that had landed them there, perhaps independently, and which could, at any moment, make them disappear. On the lowest shelf, four plastic animals were lined up as if they were fleeing toward the wall: two identical seals, one black penguin, and one slightly larger penguin with a white chest (as I understand it, these have a special name). At the center of the shelf, a clock in a square frame had stopped telling time at twenty-seven minutes past ten one day. Propped up on the clock, which was the only thing that kept it from falling over entirely, was a small paperback titled *What Napoleon's Biographers Don't Say* and, on the other side, perhaps suggesting the existence of an alternate astronomical hemisphere or temporal dimension, the spine of a book from the same series read *Adam, Eve, and I.*

No one said a word. The Cuban daughter and her Dominican mother: Felix felt an urge to explore the subject, which meant he needed to devise a way to start the conversation. But the woman, wanting to avoid the question that her infallible instinct, the fruit of repeated experience, told her was imminent, abruptly lifted the phone to her ear and started talking as if she were picking up a conversation where she had left off. She was explaining what had happened to some money that had gone missing. Felix thought she seemed completely absorbed in her story: she had put the money in her pocket and then forgotten about it; a few days later, she got the pants back from the laundry and the money was gone. (Right then she turned back to the girl and whispered "Go, Laene," or something like that, making a gesture in Felix's general direction.) As a result, Felix missed the rest of the conversation but did learn the name of the girl, who showed him to his room without needing to say a word.

They walked over to the elevator, a heavy machine proportional to the building on the outside but startlingly small on the inside; its capacity was severely reduced by the layers of wood and Formica patches that covered its walls. With more than one person inside, it was impossible to turn around to close the door. And so Laene and Felix ended up face to face, their bodies almost touching. The amused expression on the girl's face embarrassed him, but he found a solution right away and stepped out of the elevator to enter again, backwards. These small movements, coupled with the proximity of their bodies, seemed to Felix like the steps of a delicate, unintentional dance. He tried to start a conversation that might lead to the topic that so interested him, but they reached the second floor before he could muster any small talk. Now they were standing in a different hallway, one with too many twists and turns, and walls that seemed fake at first glance. As he walked, Felix remembered the uniform, endearing world (ramshackle cantinas, dimly-lit rooms with walls caked in years of dirt, shoddy furniture, violent heat, and stifled laughter or, rather, whimpers of distress) at guesthouses overlooking the warm sea. He remembered all this and felt both a deep sadness at having recovered it when he least expected, and a rush of satisfaction at identifying his nostalgia. The feeling was so strong that he was suddenly inspired to announce his intention to take the room. Moments later, Laene opened the door and Felix, predictably, realized he'd made a mistake. Not that it really mattered. Each time he used the elevator over the next few days, he would wonder about the Formica panels and the space they occupied; whether there was anything behind them, if they were hiding something.

Not forgetting would require a sketch, descriptions jotted on a loose sheet of paper. The room is long and narrow; its walls are painted an indeterminate shade of blue that sometimes, momentarily and depending on the daylight that doesn't always find its way inside, turns an unexpected ultramarine. The furnishings consist of a twin bed, a small nightstand, a chair, and a wardrobe with six drawers, two shelves, and no door; this list should also include, because they are in the room, a small sink with an old mirror hanging on the wall above it and, in one corner, a bathroom squeezed in between two partitions or thin walls that don't reach the ceiling. (At first glance, most people probably mistake it for, say, a dressing room.) The bathroom has no door; instead, there is a white arch (decorated, incidentally, as if it were the entrance to a sacred vault) and a plastic curtain hanging from large, heavy rings that make it difficult to open or close. There is another curtain in the room, this one an intensely orange sheet of rubber, which covers the window (small and sealed shut, with dirty, damaged panes) that faces, from beside the sink, the interior of the dilapidated building. Beyond its squalor and stagnant air and the chipping paint on the walls, however, the room produces a vague sense of melancholy, as if it were real and artificial at the same time; simple yet unnecessarily complicated, due to the enormous window set into the divider that marks off the bathroom. The window is made of thick, vertically striped glass and is too big to

15

look like a porthole; its heavy frame, adorned with branches and buds that unintentionally evoke funeral wreaths and are painted white in a futile attempt to suggest transatlantic journeys, condemns the room to producing sensations of intentional inappropriateness or studied ugliness. Finally, as if it were a postscript to a report, the room's third curtain should be mentioned: made of the thinnest turquoise plastic, it hangs perpendicular to the toilet, enclosing the solitary shower.

Felix spends hours lying in bed, his eyes fixed on the big round window. Later, when he decides it is time to go out, he stands and gets ready to take a long, aimless walk. On the morning of the third day, his room loses power. He has always felt prepared to suffer adversity, is even predisposed to it, so blackouts never surprise him. Still, he goes down to the reception desk to inquire about it and discovers on the way that the elevator is working and the solitary hallway lights are lit. Laene is reading a women's magazine. At her back, her mute audience of miniature animals continues its eternal exodus toward the wall. She doesn't know anything about it, but says, weighing her words with what seems like newfound care, that she'll call the gentleman who does maintenance on the building. Felix leaves; when he is out in the street he remembers those cities by the warm sea, and how everyone is a "Lady" or a "Gentleman" there. When he returns that night, he will find that the power is still out. Several days go by like this and Felix stops asking for it to be fixed; in a way, he takes it as the new terms that the Samich Guesthouse is able to offer for his stay, whether the women in charge like it or not. His room is almost as dark during the day as it is at night (another element, along with its vibrant colors and precarious narrowness that Felix associates with rooms on that other sea), and he can't tell whether he can bear all this thanks to the nostalgia that the guesthouse and its many challenges awaken in him, or if it is his penchant for infinite tolerance, which is strongest in the face of adversity.

Another time, I received a thick, rough sheet of paper stamped with the logo of a hotel in Moscow. The place was called "Salgado" and the whole thing seemed like another one of Felix's typical quirks, the way he revels in any extravagant detail. I was surprised by the heading, which was also printed in Cyrillic, though it woud have been stranger had it not been. There was the name, the word "Hotel," and what was almost certainly the address; I don't know why it occurred to me to associate the duplication of text on that sheet of paper with conversion tables for magnitudes, distances, and temperatures, but I thought that if two forms of writing occupied the space of a single page, it was so one could expose the uselessness or redundancy of the other and, in so doing, reveal not only its limitations but also, in a sense, its arrogance. I imagined Felix in Moscow's exaggerated cold, which was, I thought, just as measurable as any other, but was nonetheless different in substance. The hotel's logo was stamped on the right side of the letterhead: instead of a coat of arms without, perhaps, much history behind it, they had chosen the figure of a door standing ajar. Years ago, in another of his brief missives, Felix had admitted that every time he arrived at a hotel he'd always think it was closed or had no vacancies, or that they would deny him lodging for some other reason. I gathered that, on this occasion, the image had seemed auspicious; because of it, the bastion that was the Hotel Salgado promised not to be entirely impenetrable.

I remember that in the very first line, before summarizing his recent movements and tossing out an enigmatic quip, Felix announced, "The Hotel Salgado opened its doors to me." I don't know why, but I found it strange that the door opened to the left; this detail transformed a simple and forgettable logo into a mystery. I thought that any door left open so slightly, and in that direction, could only lead to a hidden place. I imagined the dark night and the city's cold, empty streets, and in that innocent commercial drawing I saw the sign of an imminent yet unlikely danger, as if a previous unknown order had decided to reveal itself without any prior indications or beliefs that might have served as a warning.

I should mention that I saw in the Hotel Salgado's logo evidence of the arbitrary danger to which the world subjects us. Sometimes we submit to this danger enthusiastically, other times we do so unconsciously, fearfully, or even with resigned consent. The Hotel Salgado invited you in; there was no sense of obligation to it, but in Russia, as in most countries, a foreigner probably doesn't encounter too many open doors. It was one possibility: just as Felix had, at the sight of that open door, given in to its careless welcome, from another perspective, there was probably very little about that welcome, which probably concealed a deadly trap, that was careless. It seemed like a typical ploy awaiting its next hapless victim, a snare set of its own accord. Following some deep-seated animal, or even human, drive, the victim submits himself to whatever might come, understanding that this "arbitrary danger" is the risk one assumes by living. For its part, the Hotel Salgado—probably without any malicious intent—innocently offered the traveler protection and shelter, though with the implicit warning that under certain conditions their haven might become a living hell. As is clear by now, I should acknowledge that when I received his letter years ago, I believed Felix was exposed to more than one danger. This idea occupied my thoughts for several days without ever actually worrying me. There was little I could do, after all, and the way Felix chose to make his presence felt— always unexpectedly, and making it clear that he was subject both to his haste and to some formless directive imposed upon him, or that in any event, that something was pushing him to write a few hurried lines and to keep pressing forward—suggested to me that if Felix didn't realize what had been going on for some time already, he was at least vaguely aware of what might come to pass, that his behavior anticipated an outcome that for the time being could only be known as intuition.

There are other postcards and letters from Felix, which I keep in a yellow folder. I wrote his name on the outside, and sometimes when I stumble upon it I'm filled with anxious resentment, in which my eagerness to receive another unexpected slim envelope mingles with the disappointment of knowing that the notes I've received so far are only the smallest part of a reality concealed from me; a part that was never intended as evidence or a scale model of any given reality, but rather as a fragment, which, instead of revealing, seeks to conceal or at least confuse—like the grain of sand whose smallness makes it impossible to see the quarry. This is how I receive and keep Felix's messages, though I have no way of knowing in what spirit he sends them. As I said, I can imagine him carelessly selecting a free postcard, writing it slightly distracted, and mailing it with his mind elsewhere entirely. In any event, he must have some kind of standing reminder, some trace bit of mental energy that will tell him at some unknown future moment that it's time to send another note to let me know that everything still seems to be in order—one of those generic postulates that prop up our forgotten existence. Felix is not a cautious person, but he acts cautiously. His infallible intuition reveals what lies beneath the surface of any situation, a gift that has often made him uncomfortable but has never led him astray, and which he has always known how to use to his advantage as if it were the perfect counterbalance to his impulses, typically no more than erratic whims.

Removing himself from the cold night and the dark street, Felix steps into the Hotel Salgado; in order to do so, he carefully passes through the door, which has been left ajar. Above the reception desk in the far corner of the lobby, a lamp casts a faint light that seems on the verge of flickering out. The lampshade turns the already muted palette into a spectrum of brown, gray, and black. A servant's bell hangs nearby. Felix looks at it: it is small and solid, exactly proportional to a standard one, as if some force had shrunk it down with absolute precision. The bell had lost its clapper at some point, so they replaced it with a bolt with edges rounded (Felix decides) by extensive use, which they set on a ceramic plate decorated with traditional figures. He rings and waits. He notices that the bolt is heavy and stands out against the delicate images. The lamp leaves many of the room's corners in shadow. Felix thinks to himself that the feeble, murky light is probably meant to make the bell easier to hear, as if the darkness cleared a path for sound. He finds the lobby sad, and the weak light decidedly dreary. The light doesn't reach; it can't, Felix observes, but the thought develops into nothing and goes nowhere. When his eyes adjust, he sees one shadow glint against a darker one, the outline of some object graced by a stray beam of light, some fleeting and mysterious glimmer, perhaps from within or some unexpected illumination glancing off the surface.

Exhausted by the day's walk and stupefied by the cold that nearly froze him stiff, Felix loses track of time and surrenders to the wait. He spends an indeterminate period immersed in silence and darkness. He dreams that someone is approaching him soundlessly, like a ghost. When, a bit later, he comes to and is about to ring again, he senses movement all the way at the far end of the room. He can just barely make out the undulating motion of a white robe that dissipates and reappears as the glimmer, also hazy, of a pallid face. Something tells him that this movement is the translation of a woman's form. This is when he notices that the light doesn't reach the floor, either; it is as if the ghost ended prematurely or was floating forward with its feet behind it, in a simulation of walking. Felix feels more curiosity than suspicion or fear and hurries toward the illuminated space near the lamp to await the ghost's arrival.

His movements do not reflect his vacillation; only his constant blinking suggests a certain degree of discomfort.

There is something in the woman's expression that Felix can't identify: he is unsure whether it is embarrassment or numbness, a grimace or exhaustion distilled over the course of what he imagines was a long day. She has a round face, pale skin, and hair of an indeterminate color. He finds her face agreeable, if not terribly expressive, and is unsure whether to assign this any particular value. He observes the exaggerated whiteness of her skin and remembers the translucent porcelain of antique dolls. And then there are her almond-shaped eyes, almost colorless, which stare straight ahead (perhaps still drowsily) and do not turn toward Felix—if they do, it's too furtively for him to notice. The woman finally reaches the reception desk, places a heavy notebook on it, and begins to leaf mechanically through its pages, looking for the most recent entry. Meanwhile, Felix dives into vague memories of gothic dramas and tragedies dictated by chance. The pages flip past, revealing their uniformity; each is written in the same hand, with the same docility. She has lowered her eyes—Felix watches her eyelashes flutter when each page fans them as it passes—and he notices that they pause momentarily, registering a doubt. These movements lead Felix to two conclusions: that this woman's beauty is the ageless beauty of the automaton, and that the expression of embarrassment, numbness, or exhaustion on her face is its hallmark (that is, the evidence and cost of its existence). Still, there is something unrecognizable there, some estranging element that, he thinks, would keep him from remembering or recognizing her face in a different context.

The words she pens with pale blue ink and regular movements in the old notebook do not change in appearance or orientation when she switches into or out of Cyrillic, probably to jot down something untranslatable. The paperwork drags on; not a sound reaches them from the street and the silence of the night is so thick the two of them can hear the pen move across the page in an unevenly matched battle that seems on the verge of grinding to a halt. A question stirs in Felix: he wonders if the woman might not embody some spectral existence, the ghost of someone long trapped in those confines, a rural transplant to a city where, from what he had seen, every corner looked like a village.

The woman's shadow plunges the reception desk into even greater darkness; on its surface, blurred under protective glass, Felix sees the hotel's strange symbol for the first time. He thinks about the drawing, and about himself, and imagines himself on the other side (in the image, that is, on the outside), where he had been until a few moments earlier, and then passing through. The figure could be understood as a line dividing the page into two distinct surfaces. Felix senses he is in the presence of a simple yet decisive sign, a symbol of himself, an unexpected keyword, yet another commentary on time's dividing things into a before and an after. And he remembers having read somewhere that crossing a threshold is the most common and most fleeting way to experience eternity. Even in the darkness, there is clearly nothing on the other side of the drawing's partially open door, just a deep black interior that invades one's attention the same way that the night absorbs this hotel scene, situating it in the realm of the permanent: this will remain unchanged, we want to linger on the threshold. Meanwhile, the woman is putting all her weight behind forming her letters evenly. Felix hears the pen scrape across the paper like a knife and observes the woman in profile, her soft, downy face lit from behind. He doesn't want to be indiscreet, so he lowers his eyes to the hotel's logo; in that moment, his most recent memories blur. He moves his head slowly, so as not to be obvious about it: he wants to know if the front door matches the one in the drawing, if they have similar proportions and the same design, if they open the same way (to the same side), if their handles are identical, and so on, like in a game of spot the difference. But he can't see because of the darkness and, as often happens with events that only barely occur, each time he turns his head the most recent image, vague but certainly recoverable, dissolves. Less than a moment goes by, only as long as it takes Felix to turn forward again, but he finds the woman staring at him with her deep yet inexpressive eyes, waiting for his return. Felix senses he's done something wrong; he doesn't know how long he was looking away and guesses that she must be too tired to express her annoyance. In the midst of his silence and despair, it occurs to him that he might be the only guest in the hotel and he wonders whether this might not be a fabricated, or rather, a staged scene—orchestrated to fulfill a more or less preconceived function.

He is finally given his key and the two set in motion. This is the ceremonious phase of the stay: registering and being shown the accommodations. The reception desk, which until then had occupied a place in the background, acquires the importance of a boundary in Felix's mind. He knows that being inside the hotel means having crossed the border of reception, and that being outside means not having done that. Everything beyond, when seen from the other side, belongs to the past; in the same way, if you go out (or in, depending on the situation), everything behind you, that is, everything just recently left behind, also remains in the past. Felix is sometimes unsettled by thoughts like these, though he cannot seem to avoid them. In a way, he finds himself drawn to prologue situations, as he calls them, states in which nothing advances: transitions, waiting rooms, breaks, and wastes of time in general. Which is why he is so disturbed by those mundane circumstances that seem similar but are, in their fleeting nature, their own negation: crossing thresholds, doorways, vestibules, and also the border formed by the Hotel Salgado's reception desk. (At first, this seemed merely a passing inclination, but it turned out to be a chronic aspect of his disposition: for Felix, nothing is unchanging except indeterminacy itself; everything is incidental and elastic, links in a chain. The world unfolds as one long wait; as such, transitions simply foreground our condition.)

These states associated with entering and leaving hotels first took shape in a city in the provinces, where Felix had already been staying for a while. His itinerary that day had included the same things he did everywhere: a few planned strolls and others without any discernible aim, leaving plenty of time set aside for delays, extravagant detours provoked by unexpected curiosities or certain preferences, or for simply falling into an exhausted stupor. That morning he took inventory of the things he would bring with him before leaving the room; this was his way of organizing the journey's vicissitudes, which he could not anticipate, but could sense in their possible variations. He walked down the stairs thinking the usual, and was momentarily embarrassed by his habitual thoughts, so crushingly predictable and as fleeting as sparks, but which somehow always left him in a state of surprise and suspense when they dissipated. He stepped into the street and had not made it more than a few paces before remembering that he had forgotten something.

The hotel key rack, another object of worship for Felix. He removed his key from its corresponding hook and went back to his room; as soon as he entered, he got the sensation that he had been out too long. (It was the complete silence that had quickly taken over, erasing any trace of recent activity.) Without lingering on this impression, Felix grabbed the item he'd returned for and went back over the inventory of what he was carrying. As he walked down the stairs he recalled a recent memory: a moment earlier he had caught a glimpse of the morning and that had been enough for him to take in all the day's scents mixed together, as if, after the night's stillness, the renewed movement stirred the air and jumbled its component parts. Seconds later, as Felix passed the reception desk, he would remember that he'd forgotten something else. So he went back to his room again.

In the stairwell, he wondered if there was a law (a rule, an essence, or at least some research or empirical knowledge) that governed forgetting, which sometimes dissipates quickly, or not, or even remains undiscovered for a long time. He entered his room, noticed the silence again (it rekindled, for a moment, the thought he'd just had), grabbed the item he needed, and left without delay. A sound was coming from the end of the hallway, on the other side of the wall, but Felix immediately dismissed it as an electric motor. He made it downstairs in four long strides, his mind blank despite his awareness that something unexpected was happening. As he walked by the reception desk again, he was sure an eternity was passing, as if leaving it behind him was an action that demanded to be completed in slow motion. That was when he realized something was terribly wrong; just as he was about to step into the street, he thought of something else he had forgotten.

That made three trips. He felt that both the oversights and the way he became aware of them defied comprehension because the way they'd happened one by one, as if they were regularly timed revelations or ideas, seemed to suggest carefully measured doses rather than the pure chance that shapes people's lives. The first instance of forgetting had occurred shortly after Felix passed the reception desk the first time; then, on his way out again, still in the hotel but certainly with different thoughts on his mind, the recent past was not forgotten but was instead a recovered memory—it was, let's say, an indictment of forgetting. The same thing happened when he left and returned again; by the third time he left, the whole process had begun to feel ceremonial, like a private, modest ritual one observes without being entirely sure of its steps, which have been weakened by repetition.

When he'd first taken the room, he'd seen a photo he found difficult to understand. He was generally of the opinion that pictures in hotel rooms hid something, and it seemed particularly true in this case, as the image was not a typical print of mountains or animals in one pose or another. It was a photo of two arms extended downward. Their veins stood out like twisted roots; above the hands and wrists was a lattice of strings wound back and forth, holding up two marionettes that did not appear in the image. It was noon, and the arms cast a dense vertical shadow; the strings, especially those in the left hand, were doubled by their shadows. By one of those strange effects of photography, the surface on which the puppeteer rested (maybe he was hiding or seeking shelter) was the same coarse gray as his skin, which made the presence of the strings seem to suggest someone immobilized, lying down, or facing away, in the process of being tied up. (One could imagine three bodies, or four: the marionettes, the puppeteer, and the victim who served as the backdrop.) But a pair of rolled-up white sleeves peeked out above the puppeteer's elbows at the top of the photo, where one might say the image ended, so this first impression faded as it became clear that there was no one else on that side of the photo, that the surface was just a screen in front of the puppeteer.

Felix observes the translucent hairs on the man's arms, the faint shadows on his skin, and wonders why these things draw his attention more than others, like the calloused tip of a thumb, the mark of manual labor turned into a sign of the past. Viewed from up close, the arms leave the world of scale behind and become rolling foothills. Imperfections in the skin and the light glinting unevenly off them translate into a subtly varied topography with fields, forests, and meadows at the mercy of a nearly uniform geography. Felix has an obvious thought and then a related, but less obvious one: the man with the marionettes as a puppeteer holding the strings of the world, who directs us as he pleases—without spite, but also without compassion—and then, by association, the man *as* a world, as an actual planet. (One is too small a thing to attract the behavior of others, Felix thinks; the most appropriate attitude is indifference, a future free of obstacles until the final scene of tragedy or dispersion, when the puppeteer grows tired, or forgets.)

Back at the Hotel Salgado, Felix walks to his room, a few steps behind the woman. He notices that she is wearing heavy slippers made from fox fur or something like it, without soles, like baby booties, and that her calves are wrapped in thick woolen socks. A glacial silence, the echo of distant activity, is second nature to the hotel; right away, though, he realizes that it might just be the simple absence of sound, amplified by the walls. The sound reminds Felix of a void, of depth translated into a murmur, like cliffs sucking air down to their furthest reaches. He will soon learn that the woman's name is Masha; fitting, given her lack of definition. Felix walks a bit further and glimpses a splotch of moonlight that rises at a gentle angle, then is lost in the darkness. This is when the woman pauses before climbing the stairs and waits, without turning, until she is sure that Felix—who is mildly intrigued but hasn't yet said a word—is still behind her. The climb is laborious, not because the stairs are steep, but rather due to their depth: it takes two paces to get from one step to the next. A staircase like this demands more patience than strength, Felix thinks as he observes Masha's technique of sliding her feet as far as possible across the horizontal surfaces and lifting them whenever she runs into unavoidable obstacles. They climb several flights, follow a series of hallways, and stop in front of an unmarked door. "All the rooms in the Hotel Salgado have the same door," he notes to himself and catches a trace of agreement in Masha's expression, as if she were aware of his thought.

At first glance, the room seems to be an arbitrary mix of prison cell and bedroom. There are two windows, one down by the floor and the other up high, almost like a skylight— looking out of either will require effort on Felix's part. When he manages, after several contortions, to get close to the lower window, he will see the small hours of the night in a jumble of stillness, silence, and cold that will last until morning. From there, an artificial panorama of streets opens up, as if the hotel were a ship listing to one side. The parallel and somewhat juxtaposed profiles of houses can be seen, unsteady in the faint light and fuzzy behind a thin layer of fog that is either just forming or about to lift. Beyond these, a street, visible due to the light reflecting off the wet pavement, leads away from the Hotel Salgado in a straight line.

After a while, Felix stands and sets out in search of a bathroom, which he finds hidden behind a door on a landing in the stairwell. He takes inventory of the objects inside and his first thought is that perhaps he is not the only guest in the hotel: he sees a used towel, a few battered toothbrushes, and a soap dish full of water. The light bulb, which he'd screwed into its socket to light moments earlier, was still warm, as if someone had just used it. Under these circumstances, it is easy to imagine the presence of other people. Still, something tells him it isn't true; he has the feeling he is in the presence of a simple or a complex simulation, he can't tell which, designed to convince him of a falsehood, a half-truth, or a complete fabrication. Felix imagines the routine of that other person, a man or a woman, staying in the hotel and who must have recently used the bathroom with the tranquility that characterizes solitary habits. The bottom of the tub is marked by splotches of soapy water and there are hairs distributed in an even ring around its sides.

The light hangs close to the low ceiling from a single wire; one has to move with caution to avoid bumping into it. In a big city like Moscow, this hidden—and, in its way, anonymous—bathroom is insignificant. Yet despite being a new arrival to the city and, consequently, despite his desire to see its monuments, Felix finds this small and apparently forgotten thing to be a real nucleus of meaning. Perhaps all travelers experience something similar: when he arrives somewhere new, Felix absorbs his surroundings like a sponge; later, with the passage of time, he gets acclimated to the way things work and things become less opaque, though seeing them more often does not imply understanding them any better. Felix notes the bathtub, which stands there as if yoked to another time—the old predilection for extravagant roundness, designed to satisfy a ritualistic sensuality involving helpers or witnesses—which has become a hidden and functionally useless object, given the lack of space and likely differences in the sensual inclinations of the current residents. The signs of recent use look to Felix as if they had been staged: the walls splashed and covered in steam, objects distributed evenly around the bathroom as if by accident; all indications of incomplete and obvious actions. The scene is too emphatic, he thinks, and as such speaks volumes about the simulacrum meant to draw him in.

I will put it as Felix did once, writing of other latitudes: in that "part" of the year, the cold seeps into every corner. It leaves a layer of moisture on the surface of things that vacillates between icing over and melting without ever fully reaching either state. As it settles deeper in, it freezes these objects incrementally until they are entirely at its disposal, having become, over time, potent repositories of cold. Consequently, the moisture in a peripheral—and, as mentioned earlier, small, relative to the building's proportions—bathroom like this one could not, according to Felix, indicate anything beyond the state of the enclosure itself and the periodic condensation of the air, which, under those conditions, might well have preserved day after day a scene abandoned years before. Felix was struck by this permanent renewal, insofar as it was, above all, grounded in appearances (no matter what was really going on, the cycle of cold and water would repeat in an endless sequence).

For Felix, appearances had an additional value, and when they turned back on their object—whatever they were supposed to emulate or "give the appearance" of, in this case the bathroom—to replace its purported original attributes, they seemed truer and almost tangible, even while maintaining their ephemeral and deceptive nature. Appearances were like beliefs, they belonged to the realm of opinion; shifting focus to his origins in Argentina, they were also like nationalities, which might persist but never remain the same and, over time, become a matter of choice. Later, when he is back in his room, trying to look out one of his windows, he will hear a knock at the door. He will remain motionless, silent and intrigued, afraid at being surprised in the middle of an ambiguous thought, until more knocking leaves him no choice but to ask who it is. "Masha," the woman will answer.

As he walked over to open the door, Felix realized it was the first time he'd heard her speak, that he hadn't known what her voice was like, but some special sense—over time he would come to understand it as a local logic, an extreme sensitivity backed up by a simultaneously infallible and selective intuition—told him it could only be the same person. Felix opened the door and was transformed. No human face could have provoked his expression of disillusionment, which was instead the product of his current view of the hallway; he had managed not to notice it at all moments earlier—first, when he had been led to his room, and later, on his way back from the bathroom. It was as if he were discovering, all at once, the dreariness that had been amassing in the building for decades and had suddenly been concentrated in that hallway, a labyrinth stretching endlessly in both directions without any markings on the walls, floors, or ceiling that might help someone get their bearings. A belated shudder ran through him: he wondered how he'd managed to find his room after his trip to the bathroom, and, moreover, how he was going to get back each time he went out.

The light in the hallway was barely any brighter than the faint glow in his room. Even so, Felix was momentarily blinded when he opened the door, definitive proof of his quick adaptation to this unbelievable world of shadows. He would come up with a definition, albeit a slightly forced one, for those glimmers of half-light in the Hotel Salgado that never really illuminated anything: they were the condescending gestures of the darkness, which lazily opened up trivial fissures like alms tossed out by a millionaire so people could intermittently have a bit of mostly useless light. Darkness was the rule, and light, the exception. This explains why it wasn't until a moment after opening the door that Felix saw Masha's face shining pale against the gray, looking as distracted or distant as a Russian icon.

And so, there was a moment of confusion at that indeterminate hour. On one hand, Felix did not know if the figure emerging from the darkness, bloated with layers of clothing in response to the temperature in the hallway, was simply more of what was visible, that is, unkempt and without any discernable charm, or if, on the contrary, those layers concealed a more sensual and immediate physical beauty. For her part, Masha could not be sure if Felix's curtness upon opening the door suggested an unwelcome interruption or if it was one of those sudden changes of mood that hotel patrons often have. Felix, however, does not remember this. The name Masha seemed so typical, and so well suited to this silent being, that he believed he'd already known it, as if it were information recovered from a dream, or as if a more or less familiar past had destined him to hear it. Now he realized that the moment had come, and his expression of consternation when he opened the door was the result of his just having experienced this inexplicable trance. Meanwhile, Masha wanted to say something, but did not know how. During her slow ascent, she had quietly practiced a few different ways, then settled on a fitting and melodious phrase—thoughtful, not formulaic—which had sounded perfect in the stairwell and reflected the hotel's spirit of hospitality. But Felix's curtness had made her forget it completely. Of all the different kinds of traveler, the solitary ones were the worst. Couples or groups complemented one another and tried to resolve their issues before turning to the hotel staff. Those traveling alone, however, turned every whim into a demand and treated their preferences as necessities.

Masha did not know how much longer she would go on wasting her life in the gloomy Hotel Salgado. Nothing tormented her more than those long, shallow steps that were impossible to take two at a time. With its palatial dimensions, the staircase set the stage for excessively deliberate movements: coming and going seemed to be a single confused, extravagant, gratuitously delayed action that was never fully realized; as such, going up and down the stairs was a dramatization devoid of any value beyond its own performance. This was due to the subtle inclination of the stairs, which produced a feeling of slowed movement and even of levitation. Thanks to her frequent trips between floors, Masha had gotten so used to the feeling that, even when walking on regular surfaces, she felt as if she were floating a few centimeters above the ground.

She had noticed, earlier, the confusion that the oversized staircase produced in Felix. Then his breathing had quickened as they climbed the stairs—a sign of impatience or perplexity, she thought, but certainly not of exhaustion. She could feel his breath on the back of her neck and behind her ears, cold despite his proximity and most pronounced when they found themselves on the same step, him following close behind her. Masha thought of her nighttime attire: the layers of thick woolen clothing she slept in, one irregular garment over another, which were meant to protect a nucleus, namely her body, but which also had the predictable effect of relegating it to the depths by giving it another form. Many of these garments had lost all utility beyond providing nocturnal warmth; years of use and gradual misshaping had left them completely unintelligible and only able to cover a given body part when combined with other articles of clothing in the same condition.

Though each individual garment was undefinable, this clothing was Masha's most intimate possession, not as much for its nocturnal use as for the way it concealed and, let's say, deformed her body. She knew Felix had thought something of the kind, and could not fathom how. The banal intuition that flourished in the hotel. Perhaps it was the ominous mood there, which was exasperatingly consistent and proliferated in infinite details, from the smallest and best hidden to the biggest and most obvious, and which came together in solidarity to produce a standard set of impressions among the guests. Based on her experience, Masha understood it was the power of the Hotel Salgado to induce shared ideas, outstripping the intelligence and, of course, the will of the individual, and that Felix's recent thought was proof of this.

As light and robust as a balloon made of wool, Masha understood that what she had gone to the new guest's room to say was nonsense. But she had passed the point of no return, so between delivering her message and inventing an even flimsier pretext, she opted to stick to her plan, unaware that she would completely forget what she was going to say when Felix opened the door a moment later. To her, the room seemed like the hotel's final frontier, where no one ever went and which no one ever noticed; if it did happen to pass through someone's mind, it was to inspire feelings of suspicion and reticence, as if the place were a distant, hostile territory. Masha thought there was an insurmountable difference between that part of the building and the rest, despite the fact that these two spaces were the same in a sense that seemed obvious: one was included in the other. It was, however, only a half truth that the room was far removed and suspect, or any more so than the other areas in the hotel one might visit at that moment, since the endless stairs and awkward hallways, together with all the landings, turned the whole thing into a gallery of irresolvable spatial vagaries; it felt like arriving somewhere after a long and monotonous journey without ever having left the previous place. As soon as one stepped into a space, its shape and dimensions changed spontaneously, as sometimes happened when a corner that had previously gone unnoticed would take on the—almost invariably desolate—significance of an important room.

Stairs, hallways, and unmarked doors. The Hotel Salgado had an accessible form that unfolded the deeper inside you went. A guest's first impression would be that the place was too big, and that its size translated into an unusual complexity. As an object, however, it turned out to be both multifaceted and uniform, and as such could not stand up to lengthy cataloguing. A few repeated elements were always combined in different ways. One day, Felix looked out one of the windows and jumped back in surprise. According to Masha, the hotel was a space to be penetrated, not one to wander around; it could also be added that it was a place she almost never left. Many people made the mistake of treating it as if it were just another building. In this case, the habit was still to enact the idea of what was normal; it may have been a labyrinth, but each small act of adaptation led to a general acclimation. Spaces opened before the guest without foyers or transitions, and changes might also happen this way, as if hidden forces averse to coherence were swinging their perception between rupture and continuity. In fact, those who wandered through the hotel for the first time would occasionally pause, disoriented, feeling as if the past and immediate present had faded; immersed in a torrent of contradictory impressions, they suddenly felt they were somewhere else—not anywhere in particular, just some other, unfamiliar place.

A hotel in a foreign land. Felix could imagine himself living a borrowed life there as he could almost nowhere else; a life that was decidedly his, but whose details—in this case, his odyssey in the Hotel Salgado—could easily have been assigned to another; all it would have taken was the smallest difference, being just a few minutes too early or too late, to dispel the sequence of actions that had delivered him to where he was. In hotels, he felt like a person without a past, or, rather, he felt like a person with a vague and malleable past. This was not a problem for him at all, because all he needed to do was put some, let's say, superficial piece of his life in order—the ceremonies of his morning routine, returning to his room, personal traces left on his space—to feel a new memory surge in some small part of himself. This state of transparency (being visible and also not, reducing his physical presence to the traces of his actions) was exacerbated in a hotel like the Salgado and had struck Felix right away, when he had needed to wait for Masha for an unspecified period of time and when, once registered, he'd watched her fade into the darkness behind the reception desk. Later, it was only with great effort that he had been able to see Masha signaling that he should follow her with a languid movement of her arm that Felix received somewhat dubiously. (Still, this is the most touching memory he has of Masha, her comical gesture of leaning backward with one hand extended, ready to guide him.)

The sensations Felix experienced in the Hotel Salgado, particularly when at the mercy of the cold, the deathly silence, and the murmurings of the void, surely originated with those vast enclosures that stretched far into the darkness and out of sight. He often felt he was moving through endless expanses impossible to contain in thought, which only reinforced his conviction that he was living in an abstract space that the Hotel Salgado produced—starting with its name, given the part of the world where it stood. It occurred to Felix that the concrete experience of abstraction was something that all hotels lent out, that their walls gathered secret lives, expiration dates, detachment, and intimacy. This might have been his vision, but Masha's was vastly different. For her, "hotel" practically meant "world," and the name "Salgado" was the closest thing she knew to the idea of confinement.

As if she were a chronic traveler, waking up each morning implies for Masha an effort to orient herself; she does not know where she is, or how and when she got there. This confusion lasts only a few moments, until she senses—with bitterness but also calm—that all is in order and she is right where she was when she fell asleep hours earlier. She recognizes the small square alarm clock on the nightstand and, next to it, the little polar bear, which she says is made of porcelain but is really just common clay, standing on its hind legs with its arms stretched forward as if it were moving toward an embrace. Both objects return her to a familiar world. Sometimes Masha wonders what this particular form of waking might mean; she understands that sleep and what happens during sleep cannot always be controlled, but she senses a practical inconsistency in her daily confusion, given that she has never slept anywhere but in the hotel. What other experience might her dreams be drawing on to suggest that she is sleeping somewhere else? At one point, this question made her think of previous lives (lives once lived that returned to her this way, like someone reaching out to grab another person's arm to keep them close); obviously, she also thought of parallel, borrowed, glimpsed, and secret lives, as well as other possible forms of interpolation.

Nights in the hotel were especially well suited, if not to these visits, which were unquestionably difficult to verify, then to this unfurling of thoughts. In reality, any type of mental exercise could encounter a repertoire of metaphors propitious for its development in the intricate layout of the hotel, with all its evocative spaces and half-forgotten, often shadowy zones that revealed themselves as Masha moved through it. Her memory of the hotel's proprietor is hazy: the man called Mr. Salgado giving instructions from the darkness he himself created by closing the heavy curtains that covered the windows and most of the walls in his room at dawn. She remembers her fear as a little girl when the man's words, which she could not yet even understand, would seem to emanate from nowhere, or from someone hidden behind the thick folds of the curtains. But Salgado was flat on his back in bed, his face peeking out between his fists, which gripped the embroidered cover of his eiderdown quilt. His foreign accent lent an exotic, authoritative tone to his voice, such that his frequent errors of diction and the rushed way he concluded his sentences, which always ended abruptly and menacingly, seemed like the verbal manifestation of the baroque folds of the curtains that tumultuously accompanied, hid, or buried the indefinable body of the man who gave that voice life.

Much of her connection to Salgado was, for Masha, a secret she never managed to uncover; the burden of suspicions and falsehoods protected by the passage of time, like shameful or unspeakable facts that might begin as a bygone error, but end up replacing the past. She was the first exposed to this the morning when the hotel staff, women whose responsibilities included introducing Masha to the daily labors of the place, let slip in half-phrases and euphemisms, all still confusing for an innocent girl, that she was a byproduct of his, that he had engendered her. That "he" was Salgado, his name exotic and slippery, omnipresent in his palace like a dangerous god.

The spirit that moved the maids to treat the docile young Masha this way was grounded in resentment. Glimpsing the future that awaited the girl, being Salgado's daughter, what could they look forward to as mere employees other than greater travails and gradual abandonment in this most hostile of cities. Masha remembers one afternoon, at the time of day dedicated to rest; she is half asleep in one of those typical Russian children's seats that look like modified country stools, but which is, in her memory, a miniature throne elevated to the height of the adults' table. Several servants, with their yellow bonnets and aprons tied tight, spontaneously perform a dance of submission around the table, bowing as they pass her as if she were a small, silent deity, a fount of wisdom and wishes. Then they lift her onto their shoulders and carry her, tossing her in the air and showering her with kisses so forceful that the smacking of their lips frightens her. From an early age, Masha clearly saw Salgado's wishes behind the education she received: those wishes contained a mandate of obedience and of appropriation—she was to become one with the building, to be its watchful soul, even though nothing, she realized as an adult, obliged her to do so; nothing even tied her to the hotel beyond the fact that she had spent her entire life among its indolent walls and silent rooms. Masha had no sense of loyalty, much less of belonging or ownership; just that early-morning feeling of surprise: her initial curiosity about where she was, followed immediately by her uneasiness about the possible causes of her confusion upon waking.

The sheet of letterhead from the Hotel Salgado, which I received weeks later without much surprise, came from a piece of furniture that held, among other things that might prove useful to travelers, several comforters and thick blankets made of dark fabric. The armoire was in the far corner of his room, and a tall stack of letterhead seemed to have been waiting on its lone shelf since the hotel opened. As happened whenever he stumbled across any kind of paper, Felix was immediately curious. He lifted the first sheet and felt its texture, heavy and rough like the paper of days gone by (the embellishment of the logo and lettering, discolored to an undefinable dark shade, also revealed the passage of time), then he held it at a slight

angle and discovered the trace of a pen stroke: someone had
written on top of it. He felt a rush at being in the presence of a
writing he knew nothing about. It wasn't a question of inserting
himself in someone else's life (which he would have done without hesitation), but simply of reading a message not intended for
him—or for anyone in particular, come to think of it. This was
not a forgotten, lost, or misdirected letter: it was simply the top-
ographical marks of someone's writing. Wanting to decipher it,
he held the page up to the lamp, but the light was too weak for
him to see anything. Felix felt impotent and worried he would
miss his chance to participate in something (he always hun-
gered for experiences he refused to seek out himself, preferring
instead to wait for them to materialize; as a result, they were so
rare that each frustrated attempt plunged him into pessimism
and bitterness), so he decided to wait and try in the daylight.
Until then, he needed to ensure that the marks, after so long
tucked away, would not be erased by these new conditions.

In the middle of that big, unfamiliar room, Felix imagined
a trivial message, that is, one that revealed nothing in particular; the world is full of jottings and letters of that sort—the
exceptions are those that say something of consequence, reveal
guilt, demand the truth, or confess a betrayal. Such were his
thoughts when another possibility occurred to him: it would
have been easy for the previous guest to spark his curiosity,
and Felix realized that this scenario, as if it were an alternate
ending or hidden part of the script, that is, some maneuver on
the part of a playwright or director, held much of the mysterious letter's meaning. Discovering its content was the only way

to formulate an opinion about the lines that fate had placed in his hands (or, rather, that he had rescued from the void). In any event, he decided to wait until the morning and take advantage of Moscow's daytime, which sometimes passes like a breath, to try reading it against the light. Felix imagined an endless network of scribes working in the shadows—"the scriveners of the Hotel Salgado," he thought—leaning unhurried and calm over the stack of papers, unaware of the chain to which they belonged.

I, on the other hand, thought about the partially open door and its possible connotations. That mundane insignia, that exaggeratedly domestic emblem probably meant to offer some promise of simple hospitality—and which, for that very reason, as I mentioned earlier, could easily hide some trap or surprise—might have a secondary effect on travelers, leading them to submit to its invisible control and to write nervously on the yellowed pages, obeying a command that no one ever confirmed but was nonetheless assumed upon passing through the door. Crossing that threshold was a state still present in the minds of the travelers; the hotel's entrance is like the door to their own homes, the limit or barricade beyond which they are safe and can do almost entirely as they please—but it was also, obviously, a state that was constantly renewed in the hotel's printed matter. The door-symbol was there like a veiled invitation to write, because, among other things, it was meant to establish a continuity: to write was to insert oneself, to pass through the doorway and step into the dark, but also to find refuge. This continuity might represent a transposition or a transgression, and it might even be the innocent or insidious, yet consequential, way by which the hotel established a commitment of, let's say, dubious intimacy with each guest. For the traveler, writing meant crossing that threshold again; as an action repeated allegorically, it revealed this commitment and a partial or complete surrender of free will. It occurred to me that Felix's letter might also be that, his submitting to the Hotel Salgado with the first word he wrote, still unaware he had become one of its legion of scribes. Meanwhile, I imagined Masha repeating her aerial strolls through its rooms.

When he woke hours later, wasting no time so he could take advantage of the daylight, Felix stationed himself below the upper window, which was so far above him it looked like an erratic flattened rectangle and offered only a glimpse of the city's white sky; he could never tell whether it was cloudy or clear. Felix was struck by this faint light, and understood that its uniform, muted weariness contained within it the short life of the day. As such, he saw himself confronted by a permanent fact that appeared coincidental and unpredictable. The classic image of captivity: the prisoner standing below a high, narrow window that projects a sliver of light onto his body, particularly his face, without error or excess. And so, as if under the halo of an infallible god, Felix grasped the paper he had set aside before going to bed and raised it so the light could hit it from behind. He could feel the glacial cold descending from the window and for a moment, forgetting the sheet of paper and the writing he wanted to reveal, he imagined his fingers frozen in their hesitant position; his hands, which had until moments earlier rested cozily under the blanket, and his blood, which had only just warmed, would soon begin to crystallize; he looked at the hardened, striated map of his skin, an opaque layer crackled like an old oil painting, a surface no longer connected to his numb, frozen flesh. In contrast to what was happening to his body, the hotel's letterhead seemed outrageously immune, though between his anesthetized fingers it appeared to grow thin to the point of transparency and looked as if it might crumble to dust.

He was immediately disappointed. It was just a few words written in oversized letters scattered across the page. He could forget the intimate or revelatory letter he'd hoped to find. The scale of the handwriting was not a minor point, because it made the page seem at first glance more like a poster, or maybe a note, but in any event not an especially personal object. Paradoxically, the handwriting's size also presented the greatest challenge: each letter became a long, winding journey, an endless circular sketch. Then there were the irregular pen-strokes, whose traces thinned and then reappeared, and which turned the search for a continuous line into a guessing game. At the edges of the page, where the lack of space became a problem that could have been avoided by smaller lettering, words had been written over others, going in the opposite direction. The result was a network of open curves that looked like the marks a child might make, but were too eloquent to have been made by chance, as if what had been written were trying to hide behind the writing itself. Felix remembered several artworks that seemed to have been written rather than painted;

the handwriting—unwound, flat, and inexpressive—perhaps revealed the prior life of those signs. Then there were the changes that took place in the paper's texture from one moment to the next. Even in the dim light, a pale sheen passed across the surface of the paper as it contracted against the cold. As a result, one line would be more visible than another until a shift in the frozen current inverted this impression, revealing marks that had previously been invisible. Then there was the fatigue in Felix's arm, which shook the page as if an electrical charge were running through it.

After an exhausting labor of interpretation, Felix believed he had deciphered the text, which read, more or less: "My wise friends say traveling by boat causes seasickness, but could not agree whether this is true for everyone." Felix arrived at that phrase, which he assumed to be an opening line, as the day was ending. In Moscow, the dusk was so long that it superimposed itself on the daylight, the first rays of which seemed to announce the faded brilliance of the last, as if it were a simple predictive mechanism hidden within a complex manmade object. This could be said of any day, at any latitude, but to Felix's eye that kind of light, which fell so elusively from such a distance and always seemed ready to quit, turned the passing hours into a misleading sequence with no discernable force, as if it might give up at any moment (this would merely require the right conditions, which the most arbitrary and incidental combination of circumstances seemed ready to provide). In this case, the day might suddenly be interrupted and the people waiting for the next moment in their homes, or walking back from the market with their purchases, would not be surprised: they would assume that the astronomical cycle had finally broken down after numerous failed attempts.

Anyone who saw Felix right then would think of a man touched by a ray of light, that is, somehow illuminated (this light as the only thing separating him from the empire of shadows that was his room). A polished surface glinted dully in the far corner, a weak echo turned mere suggestion, a miraculous and meager attempt to keep reproducing an invisible source of illumination. One could see the shadows interrupted around it, forming a point of suspension, or perhaps an end or a limit, that paradoxically generated more darkness than would have seemed possible at that hour of the day. Felix tried to imagine an appropriate context for the message, though its ambiguity made this difficult. He thought of a phrase pulled from a diary and inferred the state of someone about to set out to sea, or already in the middle of the uncomfortable crossing, who, taking advantage of the solitude of his cabin, jots down this neutral, but paradoxical and subtly malignant, thought. This individual is afraid of the sea, is afraid of seasickness, is even afraid of the huddled cohabitation forced on him by the journey. So he writes in his little notebook, which he always forgets to reread, defying the uselessness of his own thoughts and, more generally, the thoughts of his friends, who have offered him information that is as true as it is useless. The phrase occupies his thoughts, but Felix senses that no matter how much he might want to, or how much effort he might put into finding some concrete trace of meaning, he will eventually need to acknowledge that, as usual, little is to be gleaned from things only partially seen.

From a secret to a warning, from a confession to a joke, Felix thought of the possibilities behind the phrase, that "private proverb" or "motto," as he called it; as he considered more hypotheses (it might be the product of nostalgia, disappointment, intuition, or even compassion or anger), more limits began to form around the annotation, which slowly grew less clear and broke apart into fragments of truth. He imagined a set of partial and imperfect events, some without a beginning and some without a trajectory or an end, nearly all devoid of logic; a series of actions arranged in movable, portable, even interchangeable spaces; or, rather, like wooden domino tiles played face down. It was clearer that way, he thought, and above all more probable: the truth again showing its penchant for adaptation. But Felix would eventually remember that, whatever possible explanations might present themselves, someone had written that unique and self-contained message, and the confusion would return.

At one point, it occurred to him to wonder how the phrase would be read in another country and, similarly, how it would be written (not in the sense of another language, just that of another place), whether different words or ideas would be used and, consequently, what "wise friends," "traveling by boat," "seasickness," and "everyone" would even mean from one country to the next. In this way, new pieces were added to the game—pieces having less to do with intentionality than with the meaning of individual elements as determined by place. He remembered his hands in the window's cold, how he'd imagined them as a punished and divided surface.

Night had fallen, and the orderly murmur of the city was filtering in from outside, a noise that seemed to generate itself as if the streets were broadcasting the echo of the organization they maintained, albeit silently, in perpetual motion until the end of time, regardless of the activity of those who lived there; meanwhile, the steady hum of the hotel, that mix of inhuman silence and abyssal emptiness that joined the place to pits or caverns, seeped in through the walls. That was when Felix, still confused by the contradictory implications of the message and eager to leave on the following pages a few marks in his own hand that might, perhaps, inspire in some future person a curiosity similar to the one sparked in him; it was then that Felix encountered, in that fact, the ideal conditions to write me a letter. I don't know the deeper reasons behind it, if there are any, but like some kind of conventional symbol or maybe a common phrase I wouldn't recognize, a few lines below his comment about the Hotel Salgado opening its doors to him, Felix copied down the line about wise friends.

Most obviously, it might have been that he considered his stay at the hotel like a journey at sea, or perhaps that was generally true of his time in Moscow, a city known for being as flat as it is impenetrable. When I read the letter, I wondered if he was trying to tell me something, and if he was, what secret would merit being told in code. It could also be understood as disdain for a certain type of wisdom based on general pronouncements that prove useless in concrete situations, or it might be a nostalgic ode to friendship, the kind that evokes those typical adolescent exchanges full of sarcasm and fondness. What I mean is that I needed to find an explanation for the phrase, because I could not understand it as information. It made no sense that Felix was announcing his apprehension about a maritime voyage, nor could it have been his way of saying, "I'm fine," or "I think I'm in danger," or "this place is horrible," or anything like that; nor could it be read as "after such a long time wandering, I've finally found my place," or, to the contrary, "I still haven't found it." And so I received, probably just like Felix had, a divided and contradictory picture from that letter.

Perhaps the most predictable of his options was to destroy the paper and forget about the whole thing; at the other extreme, since Felix did not know what he should do, the most ambitious and arduous choice was to complete the task he had adopted as a mandate, that is, to join in the chain of messages. He could leave the paper where he found it, write his own message on a fresh page, or even leave the exact same phrase in his own handwriting on a new sheet of paper. In the end, he decided to combine all these options. Felix thought about the roundabout way the message was transmitted. He assumed someone had thought it up, or perhaps it had been dictated by custom. As is generally the rule with secrets, it was not clear which norms it obeyed and which laws it ignored. The eider-down quilt grazed the floor beside the tall bed; at the far corner of the room, where the ceiling came down at an angle and the walls closed in to form a kind of children's nook, or something resembling a hidden cave in which a person could slip quickly into the dark, there was an old brazier made of heavy iron that appeared to have gone unused for a long time, with a single burner that nonetheless remained surprisingly warm.

A few isolated lights appeared in the windows. Just as Felix had observed that the Hotel Salgado was disproportionately large relative to its front door, the lights he could see from his room seemed too faint, flickering, or simply too distant from one another for a huge city like Moscow. He didn't know what psychological mechanism compelled him to compare sizes and notice differences; it was an aberrant form of observation, attuned first and foremost to some supposed dissonance or incongruity. But this dissonance had proven more than once to be false, or rather, the opposite of false: completely true or natural, and as such, obvious and irrelevant. This gave him the sense that it was his perception that was maladjusted, that per-haps some old defect or cultural condition, or both, led him to this kind of thought and, let's say, sensibility. Argentina was a country of open expanses; like Australia, its name was synony-mous with space, transgression, and emptiness. Felix supposed that perhaps the contrast between this image of his country, which had been drilled into him since childhood, and his own experience of excessive density (the throngs of family members, the lack of space at his school, the overcrowding in his neigh-borhood, and so on) had produced this deviation, turning him into a perennial eyewitness to misalignments in proportions and measurements.

Felix knew the nimbus of light around cities, the glow seen at a distance by the traveler, who imagines them as beings that feed on the night under their domes of faint illumination. Now he was inside the umbral dome of Moscow, where the kingdom of night seemed to be winning the long struggle to recapture the shadows. Whoever approached the city from a distant place would see a hazy and uniquely dispersed mass at the end of the highway. The size of this splotch was disproportionate to the frailty of the glow, as if the city lacked the strength to assert itself against the surrounding darkness. In the street next to the hotel, the one his windows looked out onto, Felix could sense the humid air, the tentative fog that shrouded the night even further and reduced the few points of illumination provided by the city's streetlamps into a pitiful landscape of scattered lights caught in the chaos of their vapor halos.

He remembered the lights flickering in the dark, as if sus-pended in thin air at every intersection. A nostalgic tribute might begin this way: the humid nights in Buenos Aires, the stillness of the street, the constant tangible presence of water and half-shadow. Few things, however, seemed less reliable to him than thoughts based on his city; at some point, some-thing had been severed and not one of the situations, places, or impressions he recalled belonged in their own right to the land-scape of reality; or perhaps it was the other way around, and the present moment was translated over and over again, updating itself by erasing its own shadow, its sense of history, and the traces left on people. It was like being present for the creation of a world we know everything about, but from which, insofar as we are witnessing its birth, we are unequivocally excluded. We often think of things as being at the mercy of time's passage: objects, places, even plants and animals forgotten or stamped out while the world goes on in any of its forms, like a machine designed to self-destruct or a series of natural, self-regulating cycles. In those moments, however, Felix thought of himself as an excrescence of the earth; he thought that everything more or less followed its indifferent race toward destruction, as it always had, but that people held pride of place among all that was abandoned, all that was built and cast into this unrecognizable history. (As the poet Giannuzzi once wrote, "It seems that culture consists in / the thorough tormenting of matter.") It was not so much that Felix felt lost, part lonely and part out of place, but rather that he thought his condition—forgotten, scattered, nonexistent—was universal. As such, the idea of having a country or a hometown seemed to Felix to belong to a documentary or elective order of things, an act of faith; trajectories could be verified and one could belong to a place, but none of that translated to the sphere of reality, because countries were increasingly ephemeral geographies, appeals that had chosen to express themselves in hushed words spoken in a new language.

The humidity added a layer of fog to the darkness, thickening it and forming shadows that were hard to dispel. Standing on the chair to look out the upper window, Felix could barely see the street; on the opposite sidewalk (of which street, he wondered: the one behind the hotel, in front, or on either side) he saw a solitary pedestrian hurrying toward the corner, shielded from the cold by a large otter fur hat. Felix got down from the chair and kneeled by the lower window, through which he managed to see only the man's final steps as he navigated the frozen puddles, deft as a Cossack, before leaving the frame.

Felix wondered if there might be some meaning to this incomplete image, but his room seemed so dark and so bland, deep in the long night and that spectral hotel, that he got distracted: when he tried to picture himself in this state, he got upset and felt a certain animosity toward the city, when he discovered that much of his mood came from the indolence and neglect of that place. Felix remained on his knees by the window. Just as happens when one looks at the night sky and the stars appear inconstant, a light would sometimes disappear in the distance and reappear a little while later, reconstituting the original map. They were windows lit from within, or streetlights, or the traffic. These partial views of the broad thoroughfares seemed like unbroken strips of darkness on which headlights floated like points in constant horizontal movement, slowly and always in the same direction. Night, darkness, neglect, immensity, silence: Felix was unsure which of these supreme forces he was kneeling before. And then there was the cold, which had frozen his fingers at the other window, and which he now felt on his face as if the glass were a glacial screen.

Next he thought he would have preferred to find a set of well-preserved letters, each one in an envelope addressed in a shaky hand and faded by the passage of time, preferably opened only once, and that those letters would contain the key to one or two lives gone astray, stories of cataclysmic arguments that were, by the vagaries of luck and a few poorly chosen words, both trivial and a little bit vain. That is, the suspicion, worry, and fairly typical misunderstandings that allow for the existence of letters, arguments about some secondary aspect of what really matters. Felix was not trying to peek in on another anonymous story—he knew there were no more meanings left to discover in life—he was simply after a chance encounter with the trace of a stranger he could take as the sign of a reality that was available, but always elusive. He told himself (he tried to convince himself) that letters achieved a maximal level of abstraction, free from people, objects, and causes, and that it is possible to read them as the flank of a story that does not, in fact, go anywhere. This flank was the height of abstraction, indeterminate narratives held up only by the outline of the words that comprised them. This is why it seemed to him that those letters written by someone else for someone else, from anyone to anyone other than himself, lent him life, bestowed on him a dose of brief but intense existence.

Outside, the dirty snow gave the street a sad, bleak appearance. Though he could imagine the same thing happening every winter, Felix took this fact as a sign directed at him alone. Like the mountains of ice in his line of sight, which leaned against the walls to form small, dark glaciers, and their invisible companion, the constant cold to which the neighborhood submitted as if deep in a lethargic slumber; all this revealed, in its ostensibly natural organization, the surreptitious hand of Masha, intent like an invisible god on covering the tracks of her intervention. This suspicion was hard to confirm, since that passive being seemed incapable of devising a complex plan or having an objective beyond her daily chores, but her connection to the hotel was clearly of a mysterious nature. There, even the most banal things seemed to be linked together independent of any circumstance or person, always revealing their artificial nature, their status as something invented and immediately projected because, to put it euphemistically, they were already just another fold in the facts themselves, fully integrated into the normal course of events. This unremitting mechanism—like those beings in science fiction who generate imagined or parallel worlds that are, as such, more verifiable than reality itself—did not depend on the will of any particular person, Felix thought, but instead joined itself to Masha's acting and intentions, as if some complex truth could only express itself along the winding, patient routes of her subconscious.

After writing those few lines, having turned his back to the windows of his room and his general impressions of the streetscape, as he finished addressing the envelope (a task he associated with his idea of the present as a beginning without the intervention of experience or memories, borrowed or otherwise, as if his simplest actions were governed by a manual written for minds without a past, like his own, which only responded to direct commands), Felix felt an intense bitterness. He couldn't guess its cause, but the excitement that had filled him as he paused time and again over the page, deciphering its code as if he were storming the gates of a well-equipped mystery, that excitement had now receded, leaving behind only the dregs of a boundless sadness. It was the experience of uselessness, of weariness and emptiness. Somehow, this was the feeling that I, without yet knowing all the facts, had while reading the letter; coming from Felix, that flippant and ostensibly funny line about seasickness seemed to indicate deep anxiety and suffering. When one stopped to think about it, the details surrounding the message only appeared at first to have fallen into place by chance.

Felix's enthusiasm had been sincere, though not entirely spontaneous, since even the smallest details seemed to have been predetermined. He had begun to think about this possibility as soon as he arrived at the Hotel Salgado. As he crossed the invisible border of the reception desk, he sensed he was stepping into a different order of things, one in which time adopted a form that was at once arbitrary, as it always is, but also autonomous. It was the kind of feeling a character who arrives at a distant town or an empty hotel might have; at first, they think they have stumbled upon a closed-off, autonomous world, but before they know it they are vital cogs in its machinery.

Somewhat removed from Felix and his fickle moods, Masha was immersed in her perennial concerns. For her, it was essential to consider the hotel as a whole, to encapsulate the life of the building in a single, constant thought—which nonetheless would be activated all of a sudden—to understand the more or less mysterious way it functioned as a hotel, and the role that she, as the supposed heir to Salgado, played in its continued existence. It was clear that everything burdensome and negative had fallen to her, while the good parts, if there had ever been any, were relegated to a forgotten time. These feelings helped her give shape to a desire. Masha always tried to insert herself, even if only partially, into the lives of the travelers who less and less frequently found their way to the hotel. She understood this as a right she had earned; for her, it was the most tangible product of her dedication, and the one onto which she inscribed the most hope. The realization of this desire did not depend on her will alone, however, and while it would be fair for her to assume that she and the hotel would appear in the guests' memories in one way or another, it was a sign of Masha's vanity that her ambition was to leave an explicit mark, not so much in a bid for permanence, but rather as a way to prove, to herself above all, the concrete importance both she and the hotel could project onto the world.

In the furthest corner of Moscow, the kind of place where real tourists and travelers rarely set foot, where residents forgot all about the city in which they lived because it could be any city, a suburb indifferent to its surroundings where people would even forget the nature of their own activities or business and wander the streets wearing a blank stare; in this furthest corner of Moscow, the hotel rose up like a fortress, powerful and removed from whatever might be happening around it. Still, anyone looking at it for the first time would see one more building among many that, largely abandoned and having seen better days, housed all kinds of people simulating life and work.

One night long ago, when the late hour meant that the only sounds to be heard were whispers of the hereafter emanating from the hotel's basements and hallways, Masha found a thick bundle of money in one of the rooms. She was making her last rounds. Her route was different each day and followed no particular logic; she tended to let her thoughts wander as she absentmindedly confirmed that all was in order. Nothing ever happened; she had never discovered anything out of the ordinary and knew for a fact that she was the only one to set foot in some of those places, that everything would remain just as it was, silent and isolated, until the next time she passed through. Even so, just as she was drifting down a long hall, something unexpected caught her attention, as tends to be the case. She couldn't say what it was, but it was as if something common or familiar, yet unforeseen, had stirred her from slumber.

In that instant, Masha was distracted by the memory of a dream she'd had the night before: she was making her rounds without knowing when she had begun or if she would ever finish. This didn't matter in the dream because she could have kept walking as long as she lived, just like there was nothing unusual about the fact that the corridors, vestibules, and the external walls only went halfway up. The hotel was an enormous aerated structure held up by some unknown law of physics: not only were the columns and the top half of all the walls missing, each level also lacked a ceiling, yet somehow everything remained in place. At the same time, though it was night and the city and sky had sunk into their typical darkness, the building's interior, despite its new open form and the apparent absence of any lights, maintained the same gloomy dimness as always. Masha remembered little more of the dream; it was an endless ramble, though she couldn't even be sure of this—perhaps it was only a fleeting impression that had lasted an instant while she slept, or its vague recollection, and that instant was now amplified, by some particular effect of her sensibility as she paced the hotel, into a sequence of identical events.

As suddenly as it had come, the memory of the dream was interrupted, or continued in its mysterious way, when Masha sensed that something unexpected was happening and gave in to the urge to push open the door to the fake floor where she was making her rounds at the moment. ("Fake floor" was what people at the hotel called the lofts constructed to take advantage of the building's remarkably high ceilings. Sometimes it would be just a single room, or sometimes several would be grouped together in the same wing. In any case, they produced a sensation of claustrophobia and precariousness from which it was hard to recover. They were made from an assortment of lightweight materials, all easy to transport, so the sight of them inspired thoughts of a silent but irreversible invasion. Meanwhile, to the uninitiated these little rooms might seem like toys or miniatures: that person might believe a more human virtue lay hidden behind that assemblage of scraps. The fake floors also invited thoughts of labyrinths, networks of tunnels, stairs, and rooms set at different heights and with outrageously inconsistent dimensions. The most striking thing, though, which left the traveler with a mixture of sadness and confusion, largely because it was hard to understand at first where one was, was the feeling of being in the presence of something secret, something made in darkness and sheltered by neglect, something about which one should not speak though it served no purpose whatsoever.)

Masha opened the door and took in a mouthful of stale air that had probably been trapped within those walls for years, and which she tolerated with her customary professional resign. Nothing there set her on edge, she sensed no presence in that dark interior, only her own lack of concentration, as if she were still in the thrall of the dream she'd just remembered. A hand, which was hers, guided her toward the light switch; her shadow, projected onto the wall behind her, pushed her forward. Beside the still-made bed, she saw the inscrutable wooden table, the chair, the lamp that stuck out from the wall like a recently amputated arm, and it all reminded her of a scene staged by a person who immediately went on to forget his own work. As she moved haltingly through the room, Masha looked like one of those fabricated mutant or humanoid beings for whom perfection is the ability to assimilate with real people by imitating them with the skill of an impersonator. (The ruse is revealed by a minor slip, a slight pause, a millisecond's delay in their acting.) Masha, furthermore, believed in the superiority of artificial beings, which consisted of their capacity for compartmentalized—some might say selective—thought, like a machine's.

It goes without saying that the room was one of the most squalid in the hotel: with its reduced dimensions and its walls and ceiling slanted to the point of collapse, it conveyed something like a penitential scene. She paused in front of the wardrobe, which struck her as absurdly deep. All of its dimensions were exaggerated (it was short and squat, at once too bulky and disproportionately small), but it was its depth, its most outrageous and unusual quality, that revealed its authenticity. She warily studied its doors—their worn surface had the same archaic, undefinable air as the rest of the piece, and they were decorated with a carved flower in each corner—and said nothing. It wasn't that she was about to say something and didn't, but rather that she stopped to listen. As she stood there, isolated from everything in the middle of that room, the hotel made its presence known through the manifestation of its size, which symbolized both enclosure and depth. They were not wrong, those guests who felt they were living in a cave they would never fully know, hidden off to one side of the city; in fact, day by day they surrendered to the building, or whatever it is called, as they navigated its different levels like domesticated animals that have forgotten their former vigor. Inside the hotel there was no facsimile of the world, or any version of the world that through some complicated comparison of codes or relations confirmed or refuted it; there was simply a netherworld that sought to remain hidden as long as possible, representing itself and quietly repeating, to this end, the weary soliloquy of its song composed of structural noises and currents of air.

But what had never occurred in the other rooms did happen here, and the same imperious force that had driven her to enter now pressed her to open the wardrobe. The door seemed to be jammed; Masha tugged at it and it swung open abruptly. The impact echoed for a few moments, as was typical of the hotel's furniture, which always offered resistance. She peered into its dark interior and, seeing how deep it was, thought of those pieces used for funerals. "You could fit a corpse in here," she murmured, hearing her own voice as if it came from a different throat. As for the rest, the wardrobe creaked, barely managing to accommodate the new weight of the open doors. Masha looked into the void and saw nothing; once her eyes had gotten used to the dark, she caught the weak glimmer of something at the back of one of the shelves. Launching herself forward as if she were pouncing on live prey, she was up to her hips inside the wardrobe when her fingertips grazed a block of paper. Masha withdrew it from a sense of obligation; she thought it was a deck of cards, not that it mattered much to her, and just wanted to satisfy her curiosity and get back to her routine. As soon as it was in her hand, however, she realized it was a bundle of currency—and it seemed quite heavy and tightly packed. Nothing like that had ever happened to her before; she would occasionally find some change left behind out of convenience because it was practically worthless, dark metal coins whose sides were stained or worn down, or both, and whose edges had been mutilated by some efficient guillotine.

As an old mercantile city and the capital of many republics, in Moscow unknown currencies often had a diffuse value that fueled the fantasies of all. Radical political changes had established a new reality, one of the lasting effects of which was the confusing sensation of living a prior experience that overcame people in various situations. There were facts, words, and unspoken prohibitions with unclassifiable resonances that belonged to an inexistent social order unknown to many, but which nonetheless functioned as the erratic remainders of memory, appearing and disappearing, seemingly of their own accord. When the person who had unexpectedly found currency under the floorboards, in the lining of a jacket, or in some forgotten piece of furniture would discover it had lost its value or could no longer be exchanged for anything, which was the same thing, this excitement would be transformed into disappointment. Those bills were the door through which the world of the past, or at least the world closed off from the everyday present, peered in. In general, the possession of money was associated with secrecy, even more so if it was the result of chance: the lucky individual quickly traded elation for fear (this fear turned out to be the anticipation of the punishment he would receive if his peers found out).

In any event, the cash would always be stowed somewhere, and the person who found it would be thrilled and feel grateful for their good fortune, until their next disappointment. Money revealed its fickle, unpredictable nature once more; its abstraction didn't matter, as long as it served for something. The ideas of circulation, of possession, and wealth outmatched the reality of the currency, which in this sense acted as a facsimile. Not everyone was naïve, many people understood that the world is full of currency no longer in circulation, but no one was exempt from feeling, at some point, that they were in the presence of a magical device—divested of its powers, perhaps, but poised to recover them like a machine that might start up again at any minute. The idea of a lavish fortune preserved by destiny and made available only to her would fill Masha with joy and confirm her personal notion of justice, which was that it might be a long time coming, maybe an infinitely long time, but that it repaid the wait generously when it did arrive, even if this compensation seemed to be no more than coincidence. Felix certainly knew no one like Masha, who could wait patiently forever, even in the face of adversity. Things began to sort themselves out that night, correcting a situation that Salgado, who was probably her father, had created by taking all her worldly possessions from her.

When she examined the money—settled in under the prosaic lamp hanging from the wall, as I mentioned, like a mutilated or moribund apparatus or the tired arm of a hidden being, with the small, intensely red shade that more than one visitor must have taken as a bad omen—Masha could not tell whether it was a good thing or not that the bills were in a different language. She could read only the numbers, and the quantity of zeros she saw all over confirmed her suspicion that she had found a fortune. The colors, too, in their indefinable shades and combinations, came from different ones she remembered as sharper in real life, in everyday things, but which in these bills seemed to belong to an evasive, distorted category. Then there was the graphic dimension of the currency—the landscapes, portraits, scenes and monuments, the arches and columns, the scrolls and spires, and the flourishes at the end of the numbers and letters—adornments Masha saw as perfectly aligned with the wealth it proffered. She felt that a part of reality meant only for her, and with which she could do whatever she pleased, had just appeared, and that the money's power consisted in being its manifestation. Meanwhile, the wardrobe let out a dry creak—it was the wood, adjusting to the open doors; together with the noises of the rickety bed, sensitive to Masha's slightest movement, these sounds seemed to come from the depths, as if some subterranean being or entity were complaining about being disturbed.

As soon as she finished studying the money, she began to count it; this was her way of bonding with her mysterious and providential possession. Because that is precisely what the bundle of currency was: an invaluable, for now, possession that inspired contradictory feelings in Masha (excitement, happiness, fear, menace) and imposed a new order upon the Hotel Salgado. That room on a fake floor—one among so many abandoned rooms in that palace, built from scraps and grown shabby at what was ultimately the periphery, a room that opened onto a secondary hallway, one might say the ancillary branch of a principal hallway—that room had suddenly become the epicenter of the building and had the power to start the complicated machinery of the hotel, which had so long lay dormant. In reality, this new nucleus would center on something that was, essentially, nothing, because the hotel itself was merely an illusory mechanism that was real to only Masha and a few others who wandered, like her, with a poorly defined but ostensibly vital purpose, just as Felix would do before long, for example, or how the few other visitors did on their long journeys to rooms or bathrooms.

Masha immediately dismissed the idea of taking the money somewhere else, figuring there was nowhere in the hotel it would be safer. The reception area was no good for hiding anything, and besides, there was nowhere she could: the most prominent thing there, the front desk, which inspired awe with its stature and trust with its sturdy wood, was actually a facsimile, hollow behind its surface. This almost exclusively ornamental object did, nonetheless, convince many of the travelers who sometimes passed through of the benefits of staying at the hotel: they entertained the hope of finding in the rest of the premises the cozy security that it—somewhat makeshift, but solid—transmitted. In these dismal environs, the reception desk became a symbol of the real Russia and presented itself in the same way: coarse and hardened, yet authentic. So Masha left the money in the lost room, convinced that no one would go inside by chance. (There was, she thought, a reason it had sat there forgotten for so long.) And she decided to make two daily trips to check on the treasure, even if it disrupted her routine. Each time, she would count the money twice: first by number of bills, and then by value.

Masha easily adapted to this new habit of checking on the money; at the end of every morning and every evening she made her visits, which the aura of mystery and her vested interest turned into private ceremonies. The following week, however, as she plunged her arms into the wardrobe at midnight she found something unexpected, which she withdrew with a mix of caution and eagerness (she couldn't yet see what it was, and entertained the fantasy of its being another bundle of money). When she realized it was a book, she felt tricked and betrayed. An unfamiliar order was asserting itself, everything was falling apart. For a moment, she thought the money had vanished, or that it had never existed at all. Perhaps because she was used to doing everything alone, Masha tended to believe in the workings of chance, which included her own confusion and forgetting, rather than the intervention of other people. As such, she felt particularly defenseless at the loss of a possession, no matter how recent or providential, that she had made such an effort to take care of. Frustrated with herself, she slammed her fists several times against the wardrobe and hurled the book in no particular direction, as if she were trying to make it disappear—in her fury, she saw the light reflect off its spine as it bounced twice across the bed. She thought for a moment. She was inclined to give up and console herself with the idea that she had been the victim of her own fantasies, but some vague sense of dignity told her it wouldn't be right to accept the loss without really searching. So she dove back into the wardrobe.

Masha plunged inside with the speed of a person trying to recover something essential. To an observer, the scene might call to mind an unexpected amalgamation, the birth of a new figure: part human, part man-made object. An extraordinary event that depended on the near total darkness was unfolding, and would soon be forgotten. Masha found the bundle of money almost immediately—it had been waiting in its usual place, one shelf up—and was relieved. For a moment, she had imagined herself dispossessed and futureless, dedicating herself to the same old tasks, dreaming day after day of the providential foreigner who would spare no expense when buying her gifts, specific or non-specific things, depending on the circumstance, perhaps driven by Masha's unlikely kindness, or more probably by the air of squalor and need that surrounded her. The money would free her from this reality, though she wasn't entirely sure by what mechanism, or what action she herself would have to take. As for the rest, she could say little about the book from that distance; for example, it struck her as having many pages. She walked over to the bed to grab it, then returned to stand under a slat window that had been cut haphazardly in the furthest corner of the room, through which an artificial glimmer filtered in from outside. She managed to see its cover, in yellow and other colors; slightly to the right of center, she made out the image of a pioneer woman almost hidden behind the flag she held up with no apparent effort at all, despite the fact that it was twice her size. The wind was blowing at her and her dress rippled with the same movements as her hair, though with less energy than the flag. In Russia, books were all very similar; this one, Masha thought, would probably have been overlooked not only by the person who lost it, but also by whoever found it (she was proof of this). Masha wondered if the book and the money had belonged to the same person, and whether there was some connection between the two that she should keep in mind. But the meaning of the relationship didn't matter to her;

she simply took the book, keeping in mind the circumstances under which she had found it, as an object well suited to hiding the money. (A fairly common use for Masha, who had spent her childhood and much of her youth watching Salgado hide his savings between the pages of countless worn volumes.)

That was the extent of Masha's insight, though greater acuity might have been in order. The night had passed quickly and she needed to get back to her postponed tasks, so she stopped her thoughts right there. (It did not occur to her that the book and the money might both have belonged to Salgado.) After hurriedly distributing the bills between its pages, she ended up with a much thicker book than then one she had found. Masha felt a rare sensation of well-being: it was the first time that money had taken on a sensory dimension for her, in the form of an unrecognizable volume offering her material proof of its power to deform. Only then did she understand it was more than just a cautionary metaphor she had heard since childhood. If Masha knew an abundance, it was an abundance of scarcity or paltriness (for example, she had never seen more than three or four bills at once); for her, the money revealed a new kind of eloquence, the tangible effect of its accumulation. This effect might correspond, or not, to its actual exchange value, but in that form—and shrouded in that mystery—the money best expressed its perpetual abstract inspiration. Masha continued her twice-daily visits, but given how hard it was to remove the bills, count them, and hide them again, and given her assumption that they were safest inside the book, she ended up simply testing the volume's weight in the dark, elatedly measuring its thickness, and then leaving the room and the fake floor behind with her typical floating gait. Every now and then she would count the money, but never all of it, overwhelmed as she was by both the sight of all those bills piled in messy stacks and the difficulty of extracting them from between the book's pages.

These visits went on for a long time, though Masha began to feel less and less comfortable not having the treasure at her complete and permanent disposal. Moreover, she was tired of repeating that mechanical procedure, which had gone from being helpful to being an irritating barrier between her and the money. So, early one morning, while the building still slept like a beast that trusted in the arrival of the day, she armed herself with resolve and went to bring the book back to her room. Decisions like this one offered her relief, they allowed her to rise above the place she lived: the hotel, and the country in general, with all its pathetic and annoying details. Strangely, though, things of this nature—the treasure and her unexpected boldness, anything that deviated in the least from the norm— brought those details to mind.

The room where Masha slept was like all the others—dreary and cold—and shared their bizarre layout, with walls that were either too long or very short, creating the overall effect of a framing square; the few pieces of furniture inside never found a suitable location, much less a natural one. She had always slept there, so nothing about it seemed unusual to her. She remembered how scared she had been of the room's longest wall, the only place the bed could go, which inexplicably cut through the space on the diagonal, essentially turning it into a triangle. The wall leaned inward, forming a slight but notice-able curve, which appeared to support the weight of the entire building with a strength on the verge of giving out; she would look up at the mass hovering above her before falling asleep, convinced she was going to be crushed to death. Because of this, every night was a farewell for which she'd whisper the semi-religious imprecations she had learned from the kitchen staff. Now, despite the years that had passed, she still lay in the same bed, against the same wall, probably in the same posi-tion she'd adopted as a child. It was an uncomfortable posture: given the angle of the wall, she needed to lean forward, tilt-ing to one side. Whoever saw her for the first time would think of a staged pose, most likely one of penance, which was both gratuitously and quite modestly contorted—the position of a figurine whose most human trait is its improbability. The room had always reminded her of a cave, an impression that remained unchanged over the years, despite her being naturally accustomed to it.

Masha settled onto the bed, fanned the book upside down, shaking it to loosen its more reluctant pages, and ecstatically surveyed the money, which lay jumbled and motionless on the blanket as if it had just fallen from the sky. She thought again of providence; she might not know how the story was going to end, or if anything unusual was happening at all, she felt her-self to be in debt to something in particular, and also felt the gratuitous, and typically useless, sense of autonomy that comes with not knowing the value of what one has. So she began to count her cash, as she called it. She divided the bills and tallied endless quantities that communicated little to her simple mind. Only the night, she thought, the way it emanated silence, stillness, and mystery, could be the logical counterpoint to that accretion she couldn't quite wrap her head around. She imagined herself counting the money long into the next morning and throughout the rest of day, not because there was so much of it, but because the same idea that drove her to count it in the first place would reassert itself in her mind whenever she was about to finish. She was mortified by this unsettling fact. She blamed herself for not having noticed the gradual thinning of the book, but above all for having kept her money there; she also regretted not counting it earlier, believing that it might have made a difference, the delay now sank her into frustration and impotence; in all these negative thoughts, she saw a veiled form of chastisement. At no point did she say to herself that it was found money, so it was impossible to know whether in the past the bundle had been thicker, perhaps unmanageably so, or if for some specific reason or through some mechanism, let's say, she was in no position to imagine, the reduction had been going on for some time already. Like many people's, Masha's greed was variable: it might express itself instinctively under familiar conditions, or, as also happens, according to the limitations imposed by her environment. In that hotel, where there was practically no measure or median for anything, she experienced the loss of the money as a betrayal, something meant only to do her harm and for which the entire building was responsible. This thought and others like it would gradually fade as she grew tired. Besides, apart from counting, recounting, or reassuring herself that the book was still pretty thick, there was little she could do. So she decided to hide the money in her bed, in its traditional place under the mattress. The book would be closer at hand for her to weigh, as before, and she could start a new count whenever she wanted.

This solution put her at ease. The strong, icy wind that, during those moments of nocturnal quiet made itself felt through the walls, seemed to soften as well; something slipped back into its groove, the book returned to its channel, the money returned to its rightful guardianship, according to Masha, and the early morning promised a day full of minutes. She had never let a book rest in her hands for so long. Sometimes when she finished counting, as the bills waited in uneven stacks to be put away, she felt the temptation to see what this one was about. She was so used to her routine at work, distinguishing the travelers' spaces and belongings from those of the hotel, and so accustomed to safeguarding the money, which was the only thing she really saw as her own (so much so that she looked back on her life before the discovery with melancholy incomprehension as an empty, joyless time spent without purpose in hallways and rooms), that by some strange mental operation reading the book seemed like entering a forbidden space that did not naturally belong to her, but which beckoned nonetheless.

The book was where the money slept, where Masha had seen it tucked in, and where, she thought, investing it with a behavior she imagined to be automatic, it might even reproduce. To be interesting or real, Masha thought, the book should be about her; being written into a story was the fairest or most fitting thing that could happen to her, given her recent and ongoing hardships. She wanted to be the hero: not some docile Cinderella whose fortune is changed by a stroke of good luck, but rather a character who faces challenges, takes risks, and goes after what she wants. The book's cover featured an image suited to what she imagined for herself as a protagonist, that is, universal recognition, a victory of resolve, an ending triumphant enough to merit hoisting a flag. I want to be the hero, she thought, no matter if it's in the city or the country. She wasn't imagining a character who overcomes obstacles, she knew there were many novels like that already, but rather one who conquers her own indecision. Masha did not want her book to be about lessons learned in a traditional sense, or for it to center on one or several intrigues that are ultimately resolved. It should be the story of sentimental misadventures that were above all difficult to pin down; also of practical ones, though not to the point of overshadowing the others. Come to think of it, the novel needed to be like a tale of the high seas, but without a traveler or a journey, and should unfold in single frames of situations, or moments, displaying supposedly important aspects of her life.

Masha tried to think of an example and one came immediately to mind. She returns to her room after getting off work, exhausted from going up and down the stairs all day. She knows the hotel's few guests have all retired for the night—at most, some restless soul might make a hushed, hurried trip to the toilet—but she double locks her door, anyway. As always, from the monumental semi-concave wall behind her comes a murmur that seems to emanate from somewhere deep inside the building, and which sounds like an enormous ventilation system or an army of pigeons cooing in the eaves as they wait for morning. Masha digs around under the mattress; she is alarmed at first not to find anything, but, sliding her arm further in, she reaches the book and withdraws it with a pleased expression. This description would be incomplete if it didn't linger on Masha's hand as her small fingers grasp at the book, stretching to wrap themselves around its bulk. Their final attempt results in a victory that produces an immediate sense of elation in Masha and moves her to observe the book from different angles, savoring her success. She cannot believe she has so much money in her possession, or that it could take a form both so commanding and so well concealed.

There is a scene that Masha repeats because its outcome is consistent, because there is no risk of surprises or unexpected consequences. Repetition, she thinks, never gets the credit it deserves. Masha finds in this the security of knowing exactly what she is looking for and what she is going to find. The results of her actions are always similar, differing only slightly from one time to the next and, she can attest, from all the results the same actions might produce in the future: if she had to stop and reflect on them, the variations would range from slightly better to marginally worse, like endless byproducts of the selfsame. Thanks to this operation, things become permanent and experience evolves as a continually updated sequence: prior behaviors align with new ones, which in turn anticipate those to come. The scene: Masha half reclines on the bed, in as relaxed a position as the wall behind her allows. She opens the book with the spine facing up and watches the bills flutter down. Another pleasure, this time deferred: she hurries to free the money still trapped between the pages, wagging the book, now slim and at her disposition, back and forth. It sometimes happens that she is tempted to read it, in which case she will open to a random page and start with the first paragraph she sees. She has no idea what came before and will therefore obviously understand very little, but that's not a problem because she knows she can invent whatever she wants. It also happens sometimes that she replaces a character's name with her own, regardless of gender or any other minor detail, and assigns to the "Masha" she imagines in writing similar traits, her own vacillations, or mistakes that resonate with her. She believes the book—like all books, in general—conveys useless knowledge, though their insights are no more useless than the reality behind them. The real book, Masha knows, the one that holds her story isn't useless: the one, say, in which the yellow book associated with money appears, and in which not learning a lesson could imply a serious risk.

Masha imagines herself discovering, by accident, a secret numerical connection between the bills and the pages that shelter them. A quotient derived from lengthy calculations involving chapter and page numbers, sequences, character and word counts, as well as other values. It is a complicated science, hard to put into practice, but it endows Masha with almost limitless attributes because, perhaps somewhat predictably, it suggests the ability to multiply the money in question. No one asks how this is possible; just as happens in dreams, everyone simply accepts this outcome as inevitable. In the book, Masha remembers the privations and impoverishment of the Hotel Salgado, its cold and its chipped coins; she feels an era about to come to its ideal end, without resentment, shame, or regret. But the real Masha knows this kind of thing can only happen in novels; even if she's never read one, she understands it is possible. And so she decides to stop dreaming, to stop getting lost in the hypothetical book in her hands, and to start counting the bills she has left.

This return to herself is calming; she'd been in the grip of a primal fear, the way someone might fear the dark or the sea, grounded solely in the impossible idea of turning into a fictional character. For the first time in her life, faced with the possibility of changing her nature, at least in fiction, she is also seized by a kind of anticipatory nostalgia for the Hotel Salgado. She imagines its hallways, empty and unchanged, the building stripped of her presence, and is saddened by the loneliness that will take it over. As happens in the novel she'd like to be part of, this is a good guess: the grand building on the verge of falling apart without its guardian angel. And so, without realizing it, she has re-entered the realm of the book: having been lucky enough to find or invent the highly efficient currency press hidden between its pages—pages, moreover, on which she is a protagonist—Masha leaves the hotel behind and her memory of Salgado is profoundly changed.

Disoriented in the limbo between book and reality, she evokes the mornings of her childhood, when it was time to get out of bed. Silence reigns in her room, underscored by the occasional shout from the street or a door slamming, distant but sudden, in the hall. Masha knows that those moments were her happiest, marked by a finite and intense pleasure: emerging from sleep and glimpsing the leisurely incoherence and ineptitude of all kinds of human activity; the world a world set in motion to produce anything and everything like a machine that, once ignited, begins its mad, unstoppable operations; a world set in motion but capable of waiting for someone as insignificant as Masha. This is her memory of how she perceived those thuds, shouts from passers-by, and slamming doors. On one hand, the array of movement and activity frightened her; on the other, the fact that she was clearly removed from it all was proof of the protection the world had set aside for her. The outside world could generate any kind of facsimile, but Salgado and his legion of helpers would be sure to keep her safe.

Like the echo of those doors slamming, Masha remembers something about which she has only approximate ideas. There is a chronic guest who has been living for years in one of the most remote rooms in the hotel; to reach it requires memorizing a long and complicated route. Only a few people have managed to catch sight of him, but those who did have had a hard time erasing the image of this furtive being hidden under loose-fitting clothes, walking with hurried, jerking movements as if he were trying to get away from himself and failing. The longer he stays in the hotel, the harder it becomes to verify what is known about him: the legend spun around him confuses the marks he must have left at some point, and his unpredictable appearances, though sporadic, paradoxically produce an effect of gradual withdrawal, as if this mysterious being were returning to the indeterminacy from which he came, making use of occasional goodbyes through which he is both manifested and dissolves. A moment arrives when the hotel employees have nearly given up hope of regaining any clear indication of his presence; nonetheless, the memory refuses to fade completely—though it is not enough to fully remember him, a tiny fraction remains as a threat of forgetting—when the guest suddenly appears, multiplying his furtive, ghostly habits. In his room, in the bathroom he would use, and nearly everywhere he would appear (or, rather, disappear), defining a peripheral circuit noticed only much later, people start finding money. The amount varies, but it is always organized in impeccable bundles.

For Masha, this is where the story begins; everything posited or proven before these appearances is nothing more than a preamble, a backstory useful only for suggesting a few tenuous links to the past. Her memory tells her that it is these discoveries, as they are described in urgent detail by the maids, that began her symbiotic relationship with the world of the hotel, which, she thinks, she will always carry with her. As if the money were an essential motor, theories about the stranger materialize every morning in the kitchen just as spontaneously as the discoveries themselves, establishing and dismantling interpretations, searching for causes, proposing motivations and inventing separations. Masha listens enthralled to each version, but is surprised by what she considers to be an overly hasty sequence of explanations and arguments, which dizzies and confuses her even more. The hotel's employees are delighted with their discoveries, and Salgado wants to find a way to keep them for himself. That's the key, thinks Masha in a moment of clarity as she waits in the solitude of her room for someone to arrive with the latest update: the stories about the guest (his identity, his presence there, his words and gestures), whether real or invented, are there to establish the rightful holder of that money. This endless waiting and the desire for new—though usually boring and useless, outrageously abridged, scattered, and decidedly incomprehensible—details or stories nonetheless made it clear to Masha early on that she, too, would become one of the hotel's enslaved spirits.

An example of these stories: H, a maid who has worked for the hotel for more than twenty years. She has a husband and a son, and she lives with them in a large room that has been converted into an apartment on the fifth floor of an old, stately mansion. H is a typical character, if that means anything. When she leaves the hotel, she goes to the market to buy fish and a few onions for dinner; its stalls are nearly empty and the streets set up inside it seem deserted. Then she goes straight home, with her purchases in one hand and the small bag containing her change purse and her uniform, which she will wash before going to bed, in the other. This is the best part of her day, the intermission between the two orders that govern her life, and thanks to which she finds a simple escape: walking, looking, thinking. It sometimes happens that she gets confused and arrives home convinced that she left the hotel the day before, or the day before that, rather than moments earlier; and yet when she lays eyes on her narrow kitchen, the screen of boards and furniture that sets her son's room off from the rest of the space, and especially when she sees those incredibly high ceilings condemning her and her neighbors to eternal smallness; when all this settles in, she feels as if she hasn't left her home in years. She leaves the groceries on the table, hangs the laundry on a chair dedicated to that purpose, and sits on the bed to loosen her clothes and remove a few layers. Sometimes she pauses on her way back, when she reaches a corner where magazines and used books are displayed in the windows of a darkened shop. H lingers for a few moments, observing the titles and covers, then goes on her way. Later, as she removes her clothes without ever getting fully undressed, she will try to memorize what she has seen. Her feeling of amnesia, of a temporal rift that has turned the present into a time isolated from the immediate past, is probably due to this simple pause on the sidewalk, though there will always be some doubt about this, particularly because she doesn't stop to look every day.

By chance or destiny, H finds money twice in one day. Everyone says these discoveries are connected to the mysterious guest, but this is not as obvious to her, as she remains unconvinced that she has seen a real, though dubious, presence rather than a deceptive shadow of her own fabrication. The morning is already several hours old and one can imagine the entire country at work; nonetheless, the bustle of the city only reaches its outer limits as sporadic and weak replicas: a few passengers arriving on public transportation, vehicles dispersed at intervals. If you look closely, at some point you get the feeling of having traveled to another, any other, city and, consequently, of being in another country. H gets distracted by this idea: living somewhere else, being led into a world she knows nothing about, even if only for a little while. The first discovery occurs during this daydream. H is imagining herself in another country and is about to clean a bathroom, but as she passes through the doorway she pauses: she feels a violent breeze penetrate her skin. It is the best description she can come up with, though at first it seems inaccurate: violent breeze. What H means is a gust; the air slams against her back before passing through her body. A glimmer of light turns her around—she wants to see the tangible cause of this breeze, and in that instant the sensation abruptly ends: she only manages to catch a glimpse of a blurred figure whose human outline seemed unfinished, or about to dissolve, tackling a curve at the end of the hall as if it were vanishing under the force of its own velocity.

Though she knows little about religion, H has a deeply religious sensibility; her mind immediately turns to angels and mystical rapture, but this terrain seems a bit strenuous for her, and she finds it unlikely that any important event, no matter how surprising, would involve her. So she dismisses the episode and tackles the bathroom, focusing on her work. On the shelf to one side of the lavatory, a weathered board attached to the wall with hooks misshapen by time, where a row of open or broken soap containers left there by guests endows the room, as if this were possible, with an even greater air of neglect, H finds a bundle of currency that appears to have just come from the bank. The paper band wrapped around it, the beige color of which evokes generic memories of purchases wrapped in the market, bears two or three partially blurred stamps and a long signature written on the diagonal, as otherwise it certainly wouldn't fit. H gives the money just enough of a nudge to make it fall like a ripe piece of fruit into the cradle of her apron pocket. The bundle is not particularly heavy, but she immediately feels it as a weight that influences her movements and doubles her over. One can get used to anything, and she quickly grows accustomed to the idea of the money belonging to her: she imagines it belonged to someone else, before, but behind that before rests a long—and, in any event, unspecified—time, which turns the idea into a laborious and, above all, abstract thought, like those objects found in the sea whose provenance there is no point in establishing. For H, then, the discovery does not represent a mystery or, come to think of it, an opportunity; she approaches it with the same passivity as her survey of the covers of magazines and books on her walk home, dedicating them a tiny fraction of her mind.

Hours of silent labor follow; H and the few other employees of the hotel go about their work in different parts of the building, ignoring one another when they cross paths in the hallways, afraid, perhaps, that Salgado might catch them doing something inopportune. H's mind is still on the morning's discovery; she notices that she has adapted to her apron's new weight without realizing it. No one has ever, she tells herself, no one has ever returned to claim lost money, and that puts her mind at ease. She is still unaware, as she opens the door to one of the hotel's typical rooms a while later, that she is about to find a second bundle of currency. There is the bed pushed against the far wall, submerged in the shadows of the half-light, and the nightstand, which is neither big nor small, some unspecified number of chairs, a monumental wardrobe, a table. The size of this room, which resembles an unused lounge, leaves an impression, though more impressive is the arrangement of the furniture, which seems to be fixed in place wherever someone decided long ago, permanently but without much of a plan, creating an indifferent, accidental order that nonetheless exudes a certain solidity, or the invisible hallmark of age, which is perhaps also subject to the same passage of time. The rest of the room seems vaguely impersonal—in this it is like most hotels—and suggests negligence, or in any case desertion, surely an effect of the relation between size and precariousness presented by the Hotel Salgado.

One imagines that when the hotel was still something else, but already held the promise of what it would eventually be, and when that part of the city was similarly forecasting something other than what it would become, as an unequivocal symbol of the moment several people rushed in and deposited this furniture in the first place that occurred to them. Changes along these lines were probably made just as impulsively later on, consolidating and manifesting those actions: a chair dragged over to reach the top of another piece of furniture, the table moved to one side to take advantage of the meager light, and so on. H starts her cleaning, blind and indifferent to everything around her, accompanied by the formation of her thoughts. She walks over to the bed and prepares to make it by lifting the jumble of blankets; this is when she finds the new bundle of currency hidden in their folds, wrapped in, though a more accurate term would be cinched by, a wide strip of paper in a pale sky-blue, from which the ends of the bills spread outward, freed from its pressure. Unmade beds had stopped leaving an impression on her long before. She still viewed them as the petrification of someone's private space, a precise and inopportune photographic facsimile revealed for her alone; but unlike her reactions in the past when faced with a sordid and revealing spectacle that presented itself to her, sometimes quite violently, she didn't see them that way at all now; the sheets revealed nothing, or rather, they revealed the obvious—nocturnal episodes that H had stopped resisting, not because she knew them so well, say, from having lived them, but rather from the fatigue of running through that catalog of secrets on a daily basis. There were guests who could be recognized by the way they used the sheets; some were so unique and consistent in their behavior that it would take H only a quick glance at the bed as she entered a room to realize they had returned to the hotel after a prolonged absence.

A strange thought had occured to H as she'd pushed open the door to the room. She wondered which terms a book might use to describe her. She imagined a surreptitious foray into the bookstore: sneaking in on tiptoe and, with the help of the darkness from the street, grabbing the first book that catches her eye. Then later, as she went on to imagine, reading at the table until very late while her husband and son slept. The words would have to be unprecedented, extravagant (she was far too common as a subject to enter a book without violence). She began to think and realized she had no answer: What was it about her? How did she make herself seen? She imagined a few phrases to describe her actions, but found none of them convincing. For example: "She had barely entered the room before she sensed that something strange was happening there. She approached the bed slowly, still not understanding that the unusual silence was motive enough for suspicion. When she did, that is, when she finally perceived the complete and uninterrupted silence, she thought of a fabricated solitude; she told herself that some being had hidden itself in the room, and its caution (remaining alert in its hiding place, moving without calling attention to itself) was absorbing every normal sound, even those that came from outside."

So strange was the impact of that phrase, the shortcomings of which did not stop it from accurately describing what was going on, that H relived her experience from that morning, when an unknown being, as I was saying, passed through her; a strange mechanism of her mind led her to immediately imagine that she herself was someone else observing the adventures of the real H, who had no idea she was being watched. She compared the money, including the bundle found that morning, with her salary. The difference seemed outrageous. The exact amount she had found didn't matter, she had no idea how much it was, only that it was more; her pay would always be insignificant. Her salary had become so informal that nothing was left of it but vague references, translated into something concrete only on rare occasions, like this one, which involved a comparison that was, in any event, impossible. H could only say it was a greater quantity of cash, more, without knowing what that might represent. She touched the sky-blue band with the tips of her fingers, unsure, perhaps, of its material existence, and with a swift movement slipped it into the pocket of her apron. Without ever having made a decision, then, she had decided to take the new bundle of money. And so, even though on this second occasion she didn't see a shadow and no ghostly traveler or mysterious guest cut a path through her body, she knew this new discovery was connected to him.

Masha remembered that H had tried to explain this to the other maids the next morning, while they prepared the samovars and got breakfast ready. For her, the Hotel Salgado took shape through stories like this one, just like Salgado himself and everything that would later become her life; from that moment on, Masha will know the caution (fear, and of course veiled bitterness) with which each woman spoke about the Owner, as many of them called Salgado. H explains how she had tried to go about her business as usual the afternoon before. She had walked to the market with her purse dangling from her arm, with the same things inside it as always, that is, practically nothing except for the new visitors, that is, the bundles of money; as she walked the long blocks, her mind was on the part of the hotel where she had found them. As always, for everyone, that area seemed unreal to her, like a final frontier where things happened that would be impossible elsewhere; this influenced her understanding of the events, which, by having occurred there, not only freed her from all obligations and responsibility, but also grew indefinite and miraculous. Things could be unverifiable, even in the presence of signs or indications, and even if those things seemed clearly defined. She had placed the money on the table as soon as she arrived home, before loosening her clothes and hanging a few of them on the chair; later, she thought about her day, which might prove to be decisive in several ways. The bundles of currency stayed in their place throughout the paltry dinner that brought together husband, wife, and son. They didn't ask her a single question, and she offered no explanations. The husband had a few things that he treasured (a pair of tall leather boots, marble binoculars, the delicate but useless pin of an antique silver brooch, and so on); some of these things had already been promised to the son. Every so often he would take these objects out to shine them, and as he did, he would extol their virtues out loud and repeat the chain of events and coincidences that brought them into his hands. (The family bore witness to these ceremonies; for all three, it was something like voluntarily abandoning time until the father put his treasures away again.) But no one had shown any sign of noticing H's bundles of money on the table, and so no comment had been made. This is why H wondered, in the company of her friends and co-workers the following morning, whether the money had really existed, or if its nebulous origins might have relegated it to a murky existence, alive to a few (like her, for example, who had witnessed its appearance and taken it) but inert to the vast majority, who might see it without realizing what it was.

For his part, faced with the prospect of endlessly wandering through the unfamiliar city, Felix decided to stay in the hotel.

He had dedicated his first waking thought to the low temperature that day, though for moments he had trouble remembering
where he was. His arrival in Moscow had coincided with one
of those glacial fronts that occasionally descend on the region,
forcing people into more limited lives for a while, periods of
confinement and privation. He believed himself to be the protagonist of something special, a strange climatic event or the
beginning of a singular time. Felix felt the air on his eyelids
like a painful, heavy blanket of cold; his eyes were the only part
of his body that was exposed. A faint glow filtered in through
the window, a combination of light and darkness made it hard
to discern the hour. (Felix would boast in the days that followed
about how quickly he'd adjusted to this confusion.)

He sensed he was in a new place, which he understood
only partially and through contradictory evidence. He had a
vague memory of the night before, just enough to produce a
diffuse reminiscence. His eyes were watering and his fingers,
which had emerged from under the covers moments earlier,
were already frozen stiff; he wished it were all just a dream.
Later, when he came to and looked around the room, he discovered a strange, useless corner, where the walls bent like the
sides of a barrel, probably because of the ceiling, which angled
down toward to one end of the room. From his bed, that space
looked like part of something else: a secret passage leading to
a sanctuary or a hideout, the closed mouth of an abyss, or, as
often happens in buildings, the place where the room itself is
called into question. Felix thought of the forces twisting those

walls, and imagined that the floor and the ceiling were trying to meet somewhere outside the confines of the room. Then he had another, impossible, thought: that part of the room acted as the support for a staircase, and that the ceiling angled down as it did, deforming the walls, because the stairwell's descent also increased with the passage of time.

He thought back on children's stories and imagined himself trapped in a plastic bubble, in a fairy-tale cottage, or in a cell without measure or scale, where adult society locked away foreigners or strangers in general. For him, remembering childhood meant thinking about the country where he grew up. Before a certain moment, he had assumed that his country was an eternal scene: habits, situations, forms, and places promised to go unchanged until the end of time, but now he looked back and let's just say that whole picture seemed lost and obsolete. The most subjective part, that is, his memories and the traces left on his consciousness by the past, had aged best, and could be recovered at will and kept close at hand, while the other world, perceived in its moment as steady and unchanging, or at least as the condition or promise of continuity, had long ago turned contradictory and, ultimately, unrecognizable. There was a metaphysical element to the fact of belonging to a country; this was the element rooted in childhood. Another metaphysical element developed over time: that of individual memories. Felix thought it impossible that his compatriots reflected with any frequency on the meaning of their nationality; this vague premise, which was completely logical, but probably true of all nationalities, was nonetheless all he needed to intuit that he belonged to an increasingly undefined country. Like the colors of its flag, white and the sky-blue of a watercolor palette, the nation leaned toward transparency, able to encompass nearly everything without concealment or omission, and without ever fully showing it, either.

According to Felix, this made it the nation of the future—and, in a certain sense, the ideal country. There was, for example, the theme of the void: every writer had given in to that one. Vast geographic expanses, solitude, youth. If they were all talking about it, thought Felix, there must be some truth to it. People became predicates of the same things, shared the same food and, insofar as his country was, in its way, nonexistent (that is, was ostensibly a space without content), this profusion of expanses became a measurable value: his compatriots were metaphysical, incomplete, or invisible beings insofar as they came from a land without qualities; "unmarked" individuals, you might say, that could remain in the limbo of geography as long as nothing woke them. A lethargic and indifferent people, energetic only when it came to inflicting cruelty. As a result, the notion of reality was generally quite elastic, or inconsistent, or too generic; and, therefore, constantly up for debate. It sometimes happened that reality was the event unfolding, but all eyes would be on the thing coming to an end. When the event that was unfolding became part of the past and its immediate consequences were, therefore, unlikely to change, that was when it drew attention, never before. Fleeting ideas took shape and convinced the majority, allowing people to inhabit their particular, vaguely solipsistic worlds without realizing they were moving through a void made more palatable by abstractions. And so the comfortable existence of all was maintained. Nightmares, pain, enthusiasm, delirium, and danger floated among the community, searching for individuals in whom they could take form.

Felix had left all that behind several years earlier, and when he did, he felt he was simply facing the nature of his country. As such, it was not hard for him to adapt to that unusual morning. Now, that other time had fewer and fewer attributes. He was thinking not about his own past, which he'd lived once and for all, as he often liked to boast, but rather about the community's past, the minutiae, limits, and traces of which also seemed impossible to explain, but which he saw as the sole proof of its rachitic survival, destined only to fade. He wondered if this might not be the case in all countries, for all people. At the same time, he could never tell if his thoughts were too mercurial or fleeting to merit further attention. He tried to get out of bed, but as soon as he threw back the blanket he felt a blast of cold that stopped his breath. He couldn't move, but he didn't want to cover himself again, either: he was afraid that any touch, even the slightest, would be unbearable. He had always thought of the weather as a series of mutable episodes that could sometimes be unfavorable, but which were ultimately defined by one's experience and sensibility. Now he understood how wrong he had been: there was simply a reality beyond all measure or scale, and trying to escape it was both mad and futile. Sitting halfway up in bed, Felix analyzed his situation, not understanding how difficult it was to change; the air in his room that was making him shiver also deferred all movement, just as it did outdoors. Later he would remember that, atypically for him, he had barely been distracted during the entire ordeal. The perception of cold (the word, he thought, should be contemplation, or rather, communion, as if it were a spiritual unification), more despotic than any pain, chained him to a present without parallel time.

This is what darkness is to night, he thought, when the deepest night reaches you. He imagined the broad path cut by the cold punishing the steppe and, immersed as he was in his delirium, found it strange that after having come such a long way it hadn't yet passed. He followed this treacherous line of reasoning until he was startled by a noise at the door. Felix thought someone was about to enter, and his fear of being caught like that was more powerful than the cold. (Later, when he was in a position to look back, Felix would conclude that it was the Hotel Salgado itself that instilled fear.) Having nothing better in reach, he covered himself with the blanket, under the weight of which he could barely walk. Anyone who saw him dragging himself weakly toward the door would have thought of a person diminished in several different senses. Once there, Felix stopped to listen, adopting an attentive pose that might also have been an attitude of mortification resulting from the cold.

Aside from the currents of air he believes he is on the verge of getting used to, which sound like an army of pigeons trained to produce in unison a fearsome coo amplified in turn by the empty spaces of the hotel through which it spreads without obstacle, Felix hears nothing unusual on the other side of the door. (Noise, he says, trying to discern anything else; it seems to come from a dark, uninhabitable sub-basement, whose enslaved residents emit, as the only evidence of their existence, a collective murmur like a litany of unsynchronized echoes.) Little by little he begins to hear regular percussions coming from the long, empty hallways (the hotel's entrails, he thinks); they sound like footsteps falling in the same place, as if a powerless being, effectively immobilized, were trying in vain to move forward. So Felix leans the side of his body against the door and closes his eyes, and for a moment he doesn't know where he is.

He has pressed himself against the door to listen, but he can't feel the wood against his skin. It occurs to him that, though it assumes different forms—like silence, murmurs, currents of air, banging, or desperation—panic is the sole language of the Hotel Salgado. Not everyone gets used to this language; some people never even come to understand it. (Felix is still unsure to which group he belongs.) These forms appear as portents, foundationless warnings that never amount to anything, due in large part to their inconsistency, and trace orbits like birds of prey. A current of air makes a cooing sound, the wind slams against a window, the empty walls exacerbate the cold, and so on. Felix feels cut off from the world. It also occurs to him that the Salgado would serve perfectly as a residence for outcasts, as a hospice for the terminally ill, or as a graveyard for the living dead. A little while later, he wants to return to bed and curses the dimensions of his room. His feet are numb and he can't feel the hardness of the floor (at the mercy of his delirium, he thinks this is because it is made of liquid). Under the blanket, he begins to dress in bed, the first movements in a complex series of operations he plans to conclude with a trip to the bathroom. In this way, in just a few hours and without his really even noticing, the daily life of the Hotel Salgado has revealed itself to Felix with all its doubts, setbacks, surprises, and disappointments.

I thought one morning that it probably would have been the same for someone else. What I mean is that, in Felix's situation, someone else would have noticed the partially open door of the hotel's logo and, just as Felix did, would also have written "The Hotel Salgado opened its doors to me." This person would have gone on with their life, made decisions; but sooner or later that funny or clever phrase would reveal a bitter, premonitory quality that had previously remained hidden, and it would need to be translated differently: as the error into which the individual sinks each day and from which they have trouble emerging. I said something quite similar before: the phrase as a warning of the arbitrary danger to which the world subjects us. Now, I want to add that anyone in my position would worry about their friend just as I did upon receiving a note with that same comment. And so, just as Felix could have been someone else, an unfamiliar person, I could have been, too; I didn't arrive at this conclusion through any crisis, let's say, of subjectivity, but simply by viewing my actions as transferrable to others without any major change in their motivations or outcomes. Rarely have I been so sure of being just like everyone else, or at least of being someone whose experiences were far from unique.

Though nothing kept him from leaving the hotel, nothing compelled him to do so, either. Felix guessed that the same thing could have happened to him in any other place, but he was less sure it would be possible at any other moment. Anyway, the day would eventually come when, after making his usual rounds through the city, he would start packing his bag, ready to move on. In this, too, he was not unlike the other guests. He imagined himself gently closing the front door to the hotel with his right hand and taking his first steps into the uninhabited morning. His luggage, lighter from all the things one inevitably forgets, will hang from his left shoulder for the rest of the day. On this final stroll, this village neighborhood of Moscow and the surrounding area, which Felix would come to know quite well, would seem mysterious to him for the first time in a long while, as if both were reverting to their original nature in order to protect themselves from danger. He imagined those blocks, streets, big houses, and buildings; he pictured himself walking tirelessly, as he always did. All the components of this land-scape appeared scrambled and disjointed, lost in a concentric funneling. This was his filmic notion of travel: the dissolution and confusion of elements.

As I learned more about Felix's travels and Masha's adventures, I found that both behaved in a limited or partial way, as if the space, say, of events and situations from which they drew their practical, everyday experience and, in broader terms, their sense of reality, as if that space were incomplete and also changed day after day, sometimes auspiciously but always mysteriously, adopting a new form with different themes, people, and contrivances in general. In this way, it became a new "zone," just as accidental as the one before and with many shared elements, but always mutilated and abridged, and always just a bit stranger than before. It seemed to me that something was being withheld from both of them; something that was, on one hand, permanent—wholeness, let's say, a normal life—and on the other hand, the opposite of this: variation, the fragmentation of life itself, which is arbitrary but also universal. Perhaps it would be the same for any of the travelers or maids in the Hotel Salgado, but I have no way of knowing.

The intimate relationship that Masha and Felix had, respectively, established with the building, each with different foundations and with their own particular story behind it, reminded me of certain old books, perhaps the appropriate term would be "classics," in which a house, a city, a basement, any kind of lodging, or even a street could serve as the frame within which a life unfolds, without any real difficulty, while—in an clearly perceptible way—the scenery turns into an object, the evidence into causes, and the enigma into a representation. In these books, then, the story would be a projection of the place. Like an emblem, this place should constantly transmit meanings, because otherwise it is hard to establish continuities over time. These meanings could be more or less opposing variations (for example, it would be possible to have more than one version about the same place, stories that emphasize different meanings, and so on); nonetheless, the idea of the account as, let's say, a territorial metaphor should be retained. This explains why characters sometimes become hostages of the space they inhabit, to the extent that they are expected to assume an exemplary function. In the end, they sometimes turn into something resembling the protagonists of a fable, though that was never anyone's intention.

Anyway, this convoluted preamble is just to say that when I learned about the Hotel Salgado from my childhood friend, named Felix, whom I haven't seen in decades, and about the woman apparently in charge of the establishment, named Masha, and when I observed the little or much that each did, their varied or meager reactions, and how they cohabitated with that singular building, assigning it an autonomous life; when I saw them act on that stage, it seemed to be the most fitting, and also the most accessible, illustration of how certain people inhabit a given country. But, of course, no aspect of the Hotel Salgado is unique, and similar examples can easily be found. This was also the way I received Felix's postcards and notes: like scenes whose purpose, aside from communicating a memory or itinerary, was to propose some key to, or interpretation of, something that he—caught up in his own observations and experiencing different circumstances—had not noticed, but of which he was nonetheless, I imagine, aware.

On the rare occasions Masha left the hotel, it was to go to the market. She did this at regular intervals and considered the task an unavoidable part of her obligations. She had always preferred to go out as little and as briefly as possible; as a result, when the moment arrived for her to take on more responsibilities, she decided to make a fixed list of items and stick to it, to avoid delays and indecision while shopping. She was proud of this list, which she recited with great concentration as she walked; it had proven its worth from the very beginning, allowing her to go from one trip to the market to the next without any pressing needs or surpluses. As tends to happen, Masha suspected that in the hotel, by means of clandestine operations, or, at least, operations that were invisible to her and had secret motivations, adjustments were made so the purchases would last. There was a time when this had bothered her because it diminished the value of her calculations, and she went about trying to control every detail even more; in the end, though, she gave in to the first idea, that is, that either directly or artificially, the only fore-sight she had ever shown was still proving to be precise.

Being right so often about this, together with the power she consistently exercised over the hotel, led her to develop an inflated image of herself: she made much of very little, almost nothing, really; what I mean to say is that Masha lacked strong arguments to support her high self-esteem, but these meager qualities and reasons had organized themselves efficiently. Seeing her act when chance produced an encounter between them, or when he decided to observe her, Felix thought that Masha, as a character, was simply an imperfect being. This was probably the case with almost everyone; Felix thought that if he had the chance to work on a novel, that is, to represent himself and take a stance on an infinite number of subjective or general events, Masha would occupy the vacillating space of the incompletes—mysterious and cyclical people exiled to their lunar world. He imagined her as a fragile being, exposed to the elements and too partial, almost hindered for some unknown reason, to expose herself to fiction without risk. Despite this, she never left the fictions she encountered, and into which she immersed herself just as she was. This demanded Masha perform a labor of displacement; if she existed in real life as an incomplete, in the invented life, the one that was read, she attained a balanced symmetry. It's not that she was different from one place to another, but rather that the two worlds sought to complement one another, which gave her comfort.

Anyone who sees her walking to the market, lost in thought, probably assumes she is going over her list so as not to forget it. Later, each purchase will be an item checked off. But Masha is concerned with other things; the list is a permanent fixture she may never forget. She thinks, for example, about the infinite number of books like the one she found, about how people enter and exit them. The idea that they depend on the story's author to make this happen seems so obvious it doesn't explain anything, but the idea that they act according to their own will sounds impossible. Masha senses an explanation far removed from the other two: it is the people themselves who, once inserted into the books, give one another life and help care for one another, as a community of marginalized characters. She thinks, for example, about Felix, and what would become of him if she had not pulled him from the cold, black night when the whole city seemed to have turned its back on him. At the same time, she believes, individuals represent worlds sentenced to death, entire swaths of reality threatened and in the process of breaking apart.

She remembers, for example, a remark Felix made one morning when, probably confused and thinking that Masha was asking about his origins (in fact, the opposite was true; few things interested her less), he suggested that he wasn't entirely convinced that the country he came from existed. It wasn't that the space had disappeared or that its inhabitants had given up their language; what he meant was that nothing specific held them together, like those social gatherings that lose their purpose due to unexpected circumstances, but have to be seen through anyway. It had been a long time since "the latest news" had happened in his country; it had immediately passed out of memory, not so much because it was unexpected (though, in a sense, everything is), but rather because of its ultimate condition, for being the beginning, say, of the denouement. Somehow this circumstance had confirmed for Felix that it was reasonable to adopt an errant lifestyle, the naïve notion of creating realities or people who, despite being incomplete, might at least be an echo, albeit a distorted one, of what he left behind. As a result, that morning Masha saw herself as being an offshoot of Felix, though she had believed the opposite was true.

Markets and factories attract the footsteps of women at different hours of the day. Someone witnessing it from above would see a collective influx from the cardinal points and a gradual clustering along a few side streets, that is, along the streets adjacent to the points of concentration themselves, a waiting to be let in. These trips the women make to the market are immemorial, just like the trips the men make to work. With her gray and sometimes black clothing, which displays a broad range of both colors, surely due to the folds and additions to the different garments she wears, and outlined by the city's weighty architecture projecting its scenery of shadow and threat, Masha's silhouette seems to come from some unspecified moment in the past and to have been set in motion with its leaden gait at a moment determined by some erratic clock. One might think she is fleeing, when in fact she is in a rush; nonetheless, her pace is not particularly fast. It is this immemorial gait that imposes itself beyond Masha's conscious mind, seeming to dictate how she walks and astonishing Felix with its vaguely rustic choreography, as if it were a reminiscence struggling to surface.

Felix was sitting in a hidden spot off to one side of the hotel lobby, on a chair behind a flowering bush made of old wire and discolored paper that sprouted from a pot filled with stones. It was a place where he would occasionally kill time, secluded from the gaze of others; since no one ever passed through, at a certain point he adopted it as a place he could remain as long as he wanted, staying there hours on end. That morning, he was trying to figure out something to do when he saw Masha appear suddenly in a doorway onto the interior of the hotel and head resolutely into the street, apparently late for something, without giving him a second glance. It was one of those rare days dedicated to shopping, so her thoughts were probably already at the market. She had wrapped herself in so many layers of clothing that she must have felt relegated to her own interior, a nucleus virtually hidden under that imposing crust. On the other side of the artificial foliage, Felix felt like a prowler; maybe this is why he decided, for no particular reason, perhaps overcome by boredom, to follow her. He stood, pushed aside a branch that was blocking his path, and headed for the door, satisfied with his plan for the day. Once in the street, he watched the sky quickly cloud over at a pace that promised to cut the day even shorter. He didn't want to know where Masha was going, he just wanted to see her against a backdrop other than that of the hotel.

The chase was simultaneously obvious and real; to put it in terms appropriate to these two beings, it was also incomplete. For Felix, the experience of following someone made the streets seem narrower and more winding. Things were no better along the avenues and thoroughfares, many of outlandish proportions, a backdrop for an unsettling abyssal beauty that contrasted with the diminutive zeal of the side streets, since the sudden amplitude toppled Felix into a state of disorientation and withdrawal. And then there were the people, who filled the space in irregular quantities and flows, each one similar to the next, which made them seem more numerous. As for Masha, he lost sight of her every few moments, always as a result of his own distraction; after he'd gone a while without thinking of her, he'd locate her again, insignificant in the cold and the crowd, arduously cutting a path for herself like the solitary and almost imperceptible exertion of a little battleship. She seemed barely able to manage her heavy layers, but neither the effort, nor her exhaustion, could divert her from her purpose. After losing sight of her and finding her again for the fifth or sixth time, Felix wondered if Masha herself might not be the architect of these spontaneous and missed encounters; he was increasingly certain that she materialized at will, whenever she wanted.

Moscow isn't so big, after all, Felix thought as he watched her cross a vast avenue covered in ice; Masha appears and disappears as if the city were a plaything. More than her image, a black spot crossing the immense white, leaning forward a bit like one of those eternal walkers painted by Lowry, it was her name (simple, two syllables, as immemorial as the scene itself) that stayed in his mind for a while. It was not that he found it hard to connect the name to the person, but rather that he wondered if there might be a way for it to seem less artificial. Then he thought about the kind of effect a place like that one had on the spirit of its inhabitants. He studied the signs for a few businesses, but what surprised him most was how small the shops were, with their narrow display windows and doors. As he approached the main avenues he began seeing bigger stores; they were all practically empty, displaying assorted pieces of timeworn merchandise as only a modest, neglected museum could. Felix found scraps of pale fabric, kitchen utensils stained by eternities of disuse, discolored ribbons and buttons, decorations for the home that never made good on the happiness they promised. The objects were at a considerable distance from one another, creating lacunae on the tables and shelves that revealed the general uselessness of the display cases, an empty promise of which only the formula remained. For a moment, he thought that this merchandise, by all appearances unimportant, or dead, silent and unsalvageable, expelled from the world of objects before completing the cycle expected of them, was, nonetheless, the proof of how much was happening there. He is not sure why, but for some time now things have seemed more eloquent to him than people, or in any case, of a more lasting eloquence; he prefers to see the marks on the objects, the traces left by people, which are always material. Because, in the end, every individual is an entelechy; who knows what skill or truth they carry with them, to say nothing of emotions or thoughts.

There are streets that are more congested and the corners are as dense as a hive. As sometimes happens, Felix can't imagine where all these people came from, that is, where each of them lives, or how they coordinated themselves into what appears to be a collective performance. He thinks of enormous residential complexes, identical buildings and undifferentiated windows. He is unfamiliar with this part of the city, where no one is excluded as long as they know the right way to walk. Many approach him, trying surreptitiously to touch him as if they wanted to confirm his humanity, or his foreignness, or his material existence, which had suddenly been called into question. Felix felt trapped in a private and individual time. As happened to H when she suddenly thought she was living in a different country, Felix experiences the age-old sensation of seeing everything (even the façades of the houses which seem to tremble with the heavy footfall and rumbling of the crowd) as a theatrical set. Every person in the street has a specific destination, they all know where they are going and he, Felix, is the exception: not a temporary exception, but rather a permanent stipulation. The pavement is like a conveyor belt under his feet; he feels as if he's being transported. Immersed in this mass of pedestrians, he can barely see the little cafés from the middle of the street; all he can make out are the adornments at the tops of the buildings on either side, as if he were being pulled along by a current. For a moment, Felix's attention settles on the packages wrapped in light-colored paper that many carry under their arms, on the shopping bags made of rough fabric in indeterminate hues, which are doubtless full of food, and on the worn, indistinct purses and briefcases. Everyone is carrying something, as if their fear of the catastrophe they are all waiting for had turned into panic at the mere thought of facing that ordeal empty-handed.

Felix remembers old documentary sequences, though he can't remember when he saw them, of people moving deftly around obstacles, like brand-new automata trained to obey the commands of velocity; he remembers them because the opposite seems to happen in Moscow: people move very slowly, and each step forward is a feat of restraint designed to fulfill the only collective requirement, that is, to not violate the general slowness. The faces he exchanges glances with want to communicate something—alarm, innocence, hostility, pride—but a fraction of a second later, when he tries to fix in his mind the gesture or expression he just saw, he discovers that he has recorded the image as a sculpture, a motionless face turned into a mask, holding the same expression forever. He wonders then if perhaps they are figurines, simple pieces of boxwood masquerading in human form, whose true character is revealed only once they vanish from his sight.

He is intermittently pleased at the thought that he has adapted, having realized that the easiest thing is to give in, to lean against the crowd and move forward as if he were being carried, or, better still, as if its density were keeping him afloat. Each individual—Masha, for example—advanced like a small, mobile fortress covered in wool or furs, determined in the face of obstacles. Their clothes were mostly gray, black and brown, which, coupled with the indistinct dark color of the houses and the leaden sky, gave the whole ensemble the melancholy air of a forced march or collective privation. Felix felt surrounded by these waters, as if he were effortlessly swimming. It occurred to him that this was an easy way to belong to a country; it was a simple requirement and, in that part of the city, a daily custom. At some point in the morning, the crowd began to stir and headed out; then at the appointed hour of the afternoon it withdrew, dissolving at the street corners and disappearing until the next morning.

As such, he now considers it perfectly natural to lose sight of Masha: as a local, she is always getting mixed up with others like her; conversely, it seems strange to him that he keeps finding her again without trying to. Perhaps these signs should have made Felix question his assumptions. (Like most, he was just a person at the mercy of his beliefs and preconceptions, which often contradicted one another, and almost always came from somewhere else.) But it did not occur to him to do so, and if it did, he didn't draw any lasting conclusions from

110

the exercise. Instead, he thought that there was really nothing unique about Masha outside the hotel, she faded into the crowd like an indistinguishable anybody. Many of those making their way through that sea of people could take Masha's place: it would only require a few details in the person's clothing, like the layers of socks pulled up to different heights over her calves, a few involuntary gestures, carefully studied, and they would be ready to adopt the role of Masha. Even if it was impossible, he imagined her lost in that big city; as such, those moments when he found her again after losing her would have to be when she, no doubt afraid, regained her orientation and her confidence. Then he thought that, just as happened to H on her way home, for Masha, shopping was not just the unavoidable work of a good administrator, but also the outer edge of herself, which she was regularly made to occupy. This is why Felix felt a combination of disappointment and peace as he watched her enter the market: Masha was not lost, she would go on being herself—her obligations had, once more, won out over her indistinguishability.

The market where Masha did her shopping was as big as a stadium. It faced an equally immense plaza adorned only, aside from the cobblestones that covered its surface, by sparse rows of trees arranged off to the sides, most likely meant to mark off a space that otherwise would have seemed even larger. Felix tried to retain what he saw, subjecting each element to an exercise in repetition as if he were dealing with a badly projected film, its images skittering endlessly. The result was more or less exotic, grim, and probably exaggerated. He thought that the building must have been constructed for another use, possibly bureaucratic or military. The fantastic magnitude of its surface contradicted the modest, uniform height it had reached; this combination of immensity and incompletion, though it was hard to tell if anything was actually missing, generated a contradictory impression in anyone seeing the structure for the first time, provoking first curiosity and then disinterest. The people would withdraw into themselves, abandon their vigilance, and stand there as if they were hypnotized. Meanwhile, the lack of proportion spilled out onto its surroundings.

Past the building, Felix saw two women gathering stones from the sidewalk. He turned his eyes back to the plaza (a typical "market plaza," he thought, though in this case its scale made it decidedly atypical), and suddenly noticed that it was crisscrossed by long lines coming out of—or, rather, going into—the market after curving around, thinning out, or growing thick, depending on the conditions in that area. The four entrances that faced the plaza were also excessively large and gave the impression, due to the total lack of ornamentation on the building's façade, that they were holes created by a single violent act, probably of unexpected force, that had breached the heavy bricks previously occupying those spaces. This led him to imagine a building, at once unfinished and in the process of being rebuilt, with accidental doors and makeshift roofing, which remains standing only by virtue of time while people use it without even remembering its more or less benevolent existence. The long lines reached almost to the far end of the plaza; there, people were jumbled together and bumped into one another, reacting each time with a defensive gesture that resembled repulsion, as if they were hurrying away from a threat. That was when Felix realized that the plaza was the market's antechamber: the shoppers needed to form lines that were like tentacles attached to a hidden nucleus inside the building. Yet Masha had entered directly, as if there were no line at all. This fact, which would have caught his attention under different circumstances and he would have thought about it incessantly until he had an answer, was now registered by Felix as just one more of the strange but natural things that a foreigner might witness. He remembered that he didn't know where he was, which happened to him a lot in Moscow, and that he had no way of finding out: there were no street signs, no maps, no way of identifying one line of public transportation from another, and not even the subway stations were marked. The name of the market wasn't written anywhere, either, and he discovered that even the local businesses and artisanal shops that he had seen were, despite their garish signs adorned with simple allegories, entirely generic and lacked any distinguishing designations.

Another thing Felix observed in the market plaza was the women's passivity, or rather, their patience: the group standing in silence, absolutely still; the general absence of movement, despite the cold. The minor displacements (changing position, taking a few steps forward), the slow approach of the recently arrived, and the places they took in the end could not ultimately be considered real actions because, given the similarity in their attire, form, and body language in general, the group behaved like a collective blotch in which the movements of each element responded to a mechanism operating beyond the will of any single individual. The exception to this was the vapor each woman exhaled as proof of having a life of her own. These elements—vapor, silence, cold, stillness—seemed to Felix like an eloquent display of what could be found in that city. On the other hand, if one thing characterized Moscow, it was the number of people; the city presented itself as very busy, with a constant coming and going of people who have, Felix thought he had observed, a certain tendency to congregate around large buildings.

Because then there were the open spaces, places that at first appeared useless, where desolation reigned and only a few people ever went, walking with uncertain steps and a distracted air. The Hotel Salgado was practically on the edge of such a place, as common in Moscow as any other kind, and Felix wondered what kind of event or destiny had guided him there, or if by some coincidence he might have avoided it. He knew that he had wandered around the city for hours that first night, without the information he needed to orient himself; aside from a few general details, he can't remember anything—which is why he thinks about all that as if it had happened to someone else. He barely retained the image of the dark, interrupted every so often by a streetlight on the verge of flickering out, which had struck him as dense, like the cold, and immeasurable; then there was the glistening of the snow, its intermittent glimmer seeming to offer proof of an organism hidden within.

But that initial memory quickly lost importance, as night after night Felix was struck by the very same impressions. (When he had already been walking around blindly for a while, he had asked himself if the dark might not come from something more powerful and vast than the night, perhaps even something that preceded it and pushed it into being, that imposed its rules and modes of regulation. This question had remained with him since then, and returned in moments of despondency and reflection, like this one.) That force driving the night, Felix realized in the market plaza, is the air of the steppes, which is carried by the breeze into the city during the dark and settles into the deserted streets.

He didn't know how long her shopping might take, but Felix believed it would be a while before Masha came back out. Meanwhile, a few of the lines had advanced and new women gradually joined them. He stopped to watch and was reminded of his idea about prologue situations. As he saw it, that was what lines were. This was enough to make him feel a connection to, sense of solidarity with, those women, exposed to the elements, waiting idly for their place in line to move forward. They seemed introspective, lost in thoughts of their work or their families, prepared to wait and already knowing how long the line would take. Felix had another thought: prologue situations foreshadowed themselves. For example, the path created by a line anticipated the route each woman would travel before reaching her goal. There was a similar kind of anticipation to public transportation, with its well-defined and inalterable routes; its usefulness depended on this. The queue didn't transport anyone anywhere, but Felix had observed that many of the women decided where to stand after asking in a murmur if a given line would get them to this or that market stand, as if they were making their choice based on the destination.

The most natural thing at that point was for Felix to remember the crowded streets, the slow and disciplined walking that happens in throngs, roads thick with people like oversized lines; he also noticed the opposite, that inside the Hotel Salgado he was never certain of the route to anywhere or how to go about finding it. Predictably, the women in the plaza looked just as alike as always, which, thought Felix, was going to make recognizing Masha even harder, not to mention the fact that many of the women left the market completely transfigured, hidden behind shopping bags, boxes, or baskets somehow attached to their bodies. Masha will be hidden beneath her load, he thought, and it will be useless to try to recognize her; he also imagined that, in such a case, she was bound to head straight back to the hotel and, therefore, following her would be of little interest, as he would already know her destination.

Under fur hats and wrapped in thick clothing, the women leaving the market passed between the lines in which they had recently spent hours, ready for the next leg of their journey and alert, as if someone were watching them. Felix watched them walk away from the market with their matronly gait, alone in the immensity of the plaza and unconcerned by the raw weather. Their purchases could be seen in their purses and bulging bags, certainly a few onions and pieces of fish for dinner. Sometimes they passed right by Felix, and whenever one of them noticed he was a foreigner, she would shoot him an eloquent look, between covetous and distrustful. At one point, as he is trying to distinguish Masha among a tightly packed group moving away from him in silence, a still-young woman approaches him and, after a brief introduction, asks him for a television or a radio; afterward, she adds, they can go to her friend's house. Felix looks away and sees another woman watching them curiously from a slight distance.

For a moment, he imagines the space in the plaza occupied by the three of them as a two-room apartment brimming with furniture and fixtures. He is haggling with the one while the other tries to quiet the baby crying in her arms. Through the smallish window, he watches the flat landscape of the city shrink, as if the window were on a one-way flight and the four of them were only there to take in the new view. So much so, that when the baby stops crying the women fall silent and, in astonishing synchronicity, the four of them turn their heads toward the window, through which they see the motionless scene, slightly blurred because of the distance, of a city sunk into the cold. The woman with the child speaks quickly, perhaps so Felix won't understand her, but he imagines hearing that Boris would arrive at any moment. A few seconds go by and he hears a door: someone has entered through the other room. The strange thing is that Felix knows he is in the plaza, but on a surface that has been mysteriously selected for conversion to a small living space within an enormous residential compound. The woman standing a few meters away is the one with the baby, the "friend," and the woman right in front of him, the one with both feet planted on the flagstone opposite his, is the one who made the request, the one who is "still young." The one who appears in the doorway is, indeed, Boris, a young boy who runs to hug the mother with the baby and look at Felix from there. The two of you have been standing here talking a long time, the friend complains in her local dialect. Felix eventually gives in and agrees to buy the other one a television.

Meanwhile, just as before, there are women bent over on one of the side streets dropping stones into their bags, no more than two or three each. The mother hands the baby to Boris and goes with Felix and her friend to buy the television. Boris will remain seated on a tattered sofa with the baby in his arms, the two of them covered almost completely by a mountain of clothing and scraps of fabric in different colors. Felix and the two women walk along the empty, humid, snow-dirty streets with piles of debris on every corner. Now the space of the plaza is organized another way, to represent a small business cluttered with outdated artifacts; Felix can't determine the function of many of these, much less their usefulness. On the far wall and nearly hidden in the shadows, a stack of televisions that seems like it might topple presides over the community of appliances as if over a kingdom of silent, motionless beings. Felix and the two women wait, facing a few wooden crates with holes in their sides; the women are anxious and speak to each other in a half whisper that Felix hears intermittently, when the street goes quiet. They talk about their husbands, what jobs they have and what time they get home, where they go after they wrap up for the day, when they leave every morning, their plans for the future, accidents on the job. The wall of televisions reflects the activity on the street with a slight delay and some disobedience: a passing vehicle is a shapeless blotch slowly crossing the screens; a pedestrian is just a vertical shadow, thin and dark, that looks like it might break into pieces as it goes by. Even the three of them, standing in the space reflected by the appliances, have become a cloud of darkness floating in the middle of the screens, motionless despite their movements.

A long time goes by and they continue to wait. People sometimes come in from the street and exchange a few words with the two women, saying they've come for "small appliances" (then quickly discover they have a common acquaintance and the conversation turns to that person), but then get tired of waiting and decide to leave. Felix doesn't understand what it all means, in large part because everything there is so big it would require at least two people to move. Eventually, a shape different from the previous ones is consolidated in the main column of televisions. Unfazed, Felix and the two women watch the salesman materialize; he emerges slowly from the screens and stands in front of them. He tugs at his clothing a bit, as if he's just come from a long journey or wants to add a theatrical flourish to his appearance, and walks toward them as if they were old acquaintances. All the appliances appear to be broken, but try to hide their uselessness behind their excessive size, weight, and accessories. A radio, at least, insists the woman facing Felix, and the salesman immediately points to a pyramid of oversized wooden casings. The televisions are expensive, and Felix knows that buying one will mean the end of his time in Moscow. He is also fairly certain that none of them work, though this is not something he can say to his expectant friends. He imagines the three of them going back the way they came, struggling to carry the television through those empty streets, taking shortcuts, doubled over the whole time. Something tells him he should avoid this at all cost.

Meanwhile, the plaza goes on with its lines for the market and passive rhythm of waiting. The small space assigned to the appliance shop has filled a bit more with the arrival of the salesman, whose presence draws even more attention than Felix's. First, he imagines the wall of televisions, then he sees it; the same thing happens with the wall of radios off to the side. The young woman and her friend have come in close, he could kiss them both just by leaning forward a little. It occurs to him that, seen from the outside, by the salesman or one of the ladies in line, for example, the three of them seem to be talking about some important private matter. They are communicating, however, in a language of half words and undeveloped ideas composed of desires and reluctance. Another obstacle no one had considered is the fifteen flights of stairs they would have to climb with the television set. They stand there, thinking: the two women try to find a solution, one of them thinks about Boris and the baby, the salesman intuits where all this is headed, and Felix remembers Masha and wonders if she is done with her shopping.

In any case, noon had passed and soon it would be night. Unleashed from the north, a persistent icy breeze was beginning to blow; it collided with the cobblestones in the plaza and gathered force, catching the women still patiently waiting outside the market by surprise. Trailing Masha produced no concrete result; at the end of the day, Felix was left with a series of inconsistencies, taking stock of which demanded real effort on his part. Nonetheless, he trailed her on several occasions, each of which was similar to the others, down to its smallest and most frustrating details. The setting was certainly always the same, given Masha's invariable route, consisting of the streets between the hotel and the market, just like Felix's idle periods, the encounters followed by missed encounters, the long waits, and even the vacuous reflections constantly popping up. It was like the invented lives of artificial beings that crumble into a facsimile of apparent vitality and are ultimately conquered by weariness.

There was a secret that Felix felt compelled to uncover, but what he received instead from Masha was merely a series of actions determined by habit and devoid of any obvious content, and which were, upon closer inspection, only the appearance of activity. On the other hand, in the city (he could speak about the parts he visited), there was that copious, mechanical life that organized its habits into a chain of ephemera. I have sometimes wondered what led Felix to assume the existence of secrets that were worth uncovering, when in reality he would have had a hard time finding anything more predictable if he'd tried. Felix was convinced that one's life held, let's say, little psychological value; according to him, it was trivial, useless, and almost entirely without interiority. For this reason, one needed to complete it, or at least try to, by borrowing equally insubstantial elements from an ostensibly similar life. Hence, in part, his desire to travel. Destiny or intuition had turned that part of Moscow, the Hotel Salgado, and Masha into the network of elements that Felix needed to focus on in order to construct an image of simulated life, a being there and not; that strange presence the environment begins to see as familiar at some point, opening itself up, but never accepts as part of itself. Ultimately, this is the nature of the guest or the foreigner's life. Still, Felix did not realize that things were not determined solely by his will, which was, incidentally, pretty vague, or that the plot he wished to be a part of already included him more than he knew.

The last of the early afternoon light was fading when he left the market. The cold had turned the air blue. In the gaps between the lines of women, Masha thought she saw Felix's silhouette. This irritated her, and stoked her anger at herself for having gone out in the first place. Parts of the plaza were covered by layers of ice that looked like enormous puddles from a distance, but protected the flagstones as if they were a delicate and valuable patrimony. She always felt as if Felix were trailing her. Whenever she ran into him in the hallway, or this time, as he observed the people lined up for the market with his transfixed, but not at all innocent, air, she had the strong suspicion that the encounter was anything but coincidental. She thought about all the old doorways she needed to cross, the street with its crumbling sidewalks, and the area in general, which converted the city into a sequence of little villages, and she grew tired in advance. It was striking, how Felix had acclimated to certain local practices, for example and especially living with the cold or speaking softly, in a murmur, but she looked with a mix of pity and annoyance on the fact that he maintained the disjointed air of an imperfect or unsuitable person, despite the fact that his infinite passivity let him fold himself contentedly into any situation. Try as she might, she couldn't remember another guest like him. He immediately caught her attention when, standing in the middle of the cold, dark lobby after appearing in the middle of the night as if guided by destiny, he asked if they had a map of the city he could see. At the time, Masha had thought he didn't know where he was and—partly because she had no way of helping him, and partly to avoid starting a conversation she didn't have the energy to finish at that hour—decided not to answer.

Her purchases were heavy, so she wanted to avoid Felix. She never really knew how to react to him; as such, she opted to slip away from the plaza, hidden by the crowd. It would be a long walk back to the hotel, despite the yards and homesteads she crossed through as shortcuts; once there, her irritation would fade until the night before the next time she needed to do the shopping. With all the cargo on her back, the company of the masses thronging the street with the market stalls (an obligatory leg of the journey) was even harder to bear. In this sense, Masha was a foreigner just like Felix: she wondered why there were so many people concentrated in one place, all walking in the same direction. She told herself it couldn't be true, that something in her way of seeing things had led her to construct certain kinds of realities: people always going the same way, as if life weren't eloquent enough on its own and she needed to see it as even more uniform. Sometimes she wandered off course, but bumps and nudges from those same people returned her to her path, as if she were being escorted by an army of violent, sullen and irritable though ultimately benevolent, spirits. Masha couldn't wait to get back to her room and dedicate herself to her ritual of counting the money and, at the height of her fantasy, imagine that her dream of becoming a character had come true.

It was already night when she reached the hotel. Her arms were tired and her feet were numb; the last stretch through the dark had been the hardest, struggling to keep her balance so she didn't slip on the frozen puddles. She pushed open the door and went straight to the basement to drop off the shopping bags. Then she stood motionless for a long time with her eyes closed, gripping the edge of a bare table with both hands. She tried to go over it in her head. She hated her life, especially the day she'd just had; she hated the cold, which never left her in peace; she hated her clothes, and she hated the hotel. The more she thought about the things she hated, the tighter she gripped the edge of the table. Later, her hands would relax, which would mean her mind was gradually going blank, conquered by lethargy, until she ended up thinking about virtually nothing. It was a listless, homogeneous form of thought, approximate, like a consciousness that recounts only what is right in front of it or what it stumbles upon by chance.

A long time went by, and Felix was already back at the hotel when Masha came to. She opened her eyes and had no idea how long she'd been in the basement, source of the building's eeriest noises. The heavy thuds, which normally were buffered by several floors, suggested large pieces of metal being pushed slowly by a mechanical arm; the constant leaden scraping that seemed like chains endlessly dragged across pulleys and stone, was, in reality, an almost invisible mechanism regulated by the heating valves and ducts, by the system's temperature, or by the unsteadiness of the building's foundations. Completely isolated, Masha felt that this noise, though irregular—sometimes it slowed down as pressure accumulated until it seemed on the verge of falling silent or erupting in multiple explosions, or else it sounded like an incomprehensibly guttural horn—distorted her own notion of time, if there was such a thing, turning whatever forward movement it might have into a purely auditory experience. The sounds reached her muffled by those depths of echoes and reverberations (not just the ones she could hear right then, but also the ones that were translated, the ones she was used to hearing on the upper floors), and achieved a state of foreignness and detachment, as if it were the residue of an unverifiable circumstance; the noise from the street, on the other hand, arrived whole and full of energy despite the dampening effect of cold and, especially, the snow.

For his part, resigned to having lost Masha's trail, Felix had begun to walk away from the market. The ice forced him to move slowly; for this reason, and also because of its vast

surface, it took him a long time to cross the plaza. Sometimes, interrupting his reverie, he would notice people huddled
together for warmth on the corners of the surrounding streets.
He was constantly struck by the contradiction between the
vast, dilated spaces that turned Moscow into an endless city,
and the concentric spirit of its residents, who gathered together
as if the territory were a desert where none of them felt safe.
When he finally reached the other side of the plaza, the market
was a memory at once definite and difficult to prove: from that
distance, the afternoon shadows and soft light broke down its
imposing form into a quivering white mass that looked like the
atmospheric effect of a bright, cold day fading into night. On
the other hand, if he turned away from the plaza and looked
straight ahead, Felix could see the strange outline of a residential complex. Built on a ridge, its height made its presence all
the more noticeable.

Felix started off in that direction. He remembered other
walks, also endless. In Buenos Aires, when he used to roam the
suburbs at dawn and everything seemed to belong to a dying
world, or along the old canals of Manchester, which traced the
melancholy web of a forgotten plain fallen out of circulation,
populated by chimneys in disuse that had come to resemble
taciturn geological formations. There were few places he'd
gotten this feeling of having a territory expand as he crossed
it. Many associate this experience with nature, or rather with
wide-open spaces (the sea, flatlands, even interconnected val-
leys); for Felix, however, it was a condition specific to cities.
It seemed obvious to him that the more constructed the world,

the closer it was to crumbling, and that this expansion was just a more or less indirect, perhaps distracting and certainly nightmarish, corollary of that destruction. Strolls through the city and the suburbs proceeded incrementally (corners, gutters, plazas, lights, bridges, stop signs, and so on) while you forgot about yourself so fully that two characters, each ignorant of the other's presence, emerged: the expansion of the landscape (proliferation) and destruction (the material withdrawal or retreat of what had been constructed). Both adopted their roles as changeable beings or states, they overlapped and went on like that, perhaps not even revealing themselves, with their borrowed qualities. More than anywhere else, in certain cities Felix got the sensation that he was traveling through a body made of repetition and weariness, of forced postponement and decay. The destruction that the rain, the thaw, and the cold visited on buildings in Moscow might, in other places, be produced by humidity, heat, or wind. He would say this regarding physical conditions because the feelings inspired were often quite similar.

The residential complex was a chain of identical ten-story buildings connected at the sides—sometimes at right angles, sometimes not—to form a sinuous barrier, line, or garland hundreds of meters long. He imagined that from above it must look like a trail in search of its own form, set on the colorless earth. From a distance, though, it seemed like a truncated wall, and up close, due to the glint off its many articulations, it looked like a sleeping or moribund snake. There were a few straight, interconnected paths made of slab cement that had cracked and shifted in the cold, which Felix followed to the base of the buildings. An air of neglect filtered through its entryway, corridors, and common areas, an air of something that had ended long before, which insinuated itself in such a way that Felix wondered if he might be looking at a city that had been evacuated at some point in its long history. Off to one side, buried up to its waist in the frozen soil of an old garden, he saw the incomplete body of a plastic action figure. The figurine was raising the only arm it had left, as if it were calling in vain for help one last time before it disappeared; nonetheless, it was a scene without an end. Behind it, he saw a rusted, damaged television antenna propped against a wall next to the broken carcass of an old wooden radio. In the area where, thought Felix, the neighbors from the lower floors might have gotten together in the old days to hang their clothes out when the weather was good, hoping the sun would dry them before they froze, faint trails of steam rose up from around the worn edges of the cement slabs, dissipated, and soon died out altogether.

This was the only sign of life or activity. Felix looked up at the bare interconnected buildings without embellishments or additions, all those identical dark and corroded windows, that seemed as if they had been ready to fall for a long time but by a generous concession had decided to wait and allow the residents to save themselves and gather to wait for their collapse. He felt, however, like the only member of the audience. For a moment, he imagined he was the mutilated man calling for help from a sinking ship, and maybe because that toy was the closest thing he could find to a person, albeit a particular kind of person and long since forgotten, he felt sympathy for the figurine and a baffling, inexplicable sense of nostalgia. Perhaps the toy wasn't just trying to save itself (salvation was too basic a desire and all the apparent effort didn't guarantee a positive outcome), but was instead trying to recover a borrowed life. The affable, measured smile, which might have been meant to inspire positive qualities like temperance, optimism, and equanimity in its days as a childhood idol had become, in the figurine's current state, a completely inappropriate expression. Felix thought about those people who crumble and are happy; about those moments of appreciation one might experience in the middle of a disaster. A slave to its smile, the doll had no way of expressing its desperation, and as a result met its misfortune with a gleeful fatalism, which nonetheless revealed itself as false. Who knows what force took his other arm, thought Felix, leaving only a stump in the shape of a notch.

The light in that region, which a poet once described as viscous, perhaps due to the humidity always on the verge of freezing, shone from the west, giving the towers a ghostly aspect with areas of half-light where one could sense an even more glacial cold on its way, and other places where the illumination cast long, deformed shadows as the day drew to an end. The patches of dirt between the buildings, which perhaps had been set aside for recreation or decoration, were now completely barren and reminded Felix of the tundra, the taiga, that imprecise but generally solid idea of a wild territory battered by the severe Artic weather. He kept wandering around because he had nothing better to do, but also because he was vaguely drawn to the silence and desolation. Behind the buildings, on a small strip of barren land where the residential complex had apparently decided to create a space "out back"—maybe in reference to the place's past, or as a gesture of shame over what had happened there, that is, the construction of the towers itself—short, strangely gray weeds grow in thick, light-colored clumps that contrasted with the surprisingly dark earth. Felix was distracted by the islands of vegetation distributed according to an order that was at once improbable and impossible to define. Then he walked between them with his eyes on the ground, the cold hardness of which did not come from the temperature alone, but also from the long time that had passed since anyone set foot on it and took even just a few steps.

At one point, Felix walks away from the buildings and feels inhabited by desolation and withdrawal. Then he thinks about the Buenos Aires port as he remembers it on the day he left, sleepy places that seemed to be used sporadically, launching into feverish activity for a few hours when their turn finally came, and then falling right back into disregard. That morning, after walking with me over to some vacant warehouses and making small talk while we stared at the cobblestones, he stopped to look out across the wide river, as that low-lying estuary with no opposite bank, no visible currents, and barely any trace of maritime transit is known; despite the great void represented by all that dormant water, which slapped heavily against the piers and sluice gates as if some clumsy giant were out there splashing slowly in the distance, he felt an even greater void at his back, hovering over the city he was leaving behind, despite its complex buildings, population, and the length of its streets.

Steeped in reminiscences, he continues walking through the darkness around the residential complex with his back to the buildings, until at some point he looks up and is struck by the panorama that extends before his eyes, and to which he can't help but dedicate an ecstatic ritual of contemplation: as if it were a vast, bygone sea or the river he just recalled, a few meters ahead a huge crater stretches all the way to the horizon.

Felix stares in silence. He doesn't really know in the first place, but he needs a few moments to gather his thoughts and review (where he is, what he's doing, and so on). He's searching for the feeling this landscape might inspire, but his mind usually turns to muted vistas; the silent or invisible ones, the lacking, absent, or empty ones. He registers nothing aside from this vast and lonely depression, where life could never take root; if it were to, he thinks, it would quickly die out, leaving no trace behind. Nonetheless, this show of grandeur excites him, as if the landscape had chosen to reveal itself to him alone. Felix, who had always felt he came in last (not in the sense of taking last place, but rather of arriving last), now has the intolerable suspicion that he is the very first witness to this vastness. Something like a dream, but inverted, in that it doesn't restore the trace of any memory or affinity, but rather tells him he is occupying, right there on the edge of that crater, a space that is not only empty but also uncharted, and that, in all likelihood, he could be the first in a long line of silent visitors. Strangely, looking out over the desolate and somehow final landscape (it would be hard to imagine it as the beginning of anything), Felix notices a similarity with how things are in Moscow: situations develop as predetermined narratives—repetitive, old, even obsolete—but he experiences them as if the only meaning or justification of his physical manifestation, that is, of his body in that place and time, breathing and occupying a good deal of space, were to discover them.

Ever since arriving in that city, he has been immersed at all times in a scene too habitual and too complex to not be imposture. He thinks that of all the things he has seen, few seem less natural than that crater, with its artificial-looking and almost shadowless basin; and yet, nothing seems more authentic than the stillness of the landscape, so close to oblivion and death. The glossy sheen of its surface is simply the action of unchanging time. Felix makes out a few scattered heaps of earth, as if someone, or a small or weak but organized army, had dug haphazardly in vain, leaving little mountains of dirt distributed across its expanse. This trace of activity, as recognizable and imaginable to Felix as the efforts of a child digging in the sand at the shore, was nonetheless what lent the landscape its inhuman character; the labors of man, once reabsorbed by nature and translated into a new form, turned into their opposite or adopted the condition of antithesis, combining threat, oblivion, and warning in this murkily lunar landscape. No neglect could underscore this, no melancholy could describe it, thought Felix as he gazed at the crater. The evening light struck only one of its walls, casting an irregular shadow at his feet, jagged for long stretches at a time, from the ridge on the opposite side.

This desert made Felix realize that, without meaning or wanting to, he had discovered a limit territory. In the only sense he knew, at least, the world ended and this other territory began, with its new and unfamiliar rules. Felix gave himself over to the steppe—its depth, the sharpness of its air, its abyssal silence, and its immense scale—and again thought it strange that he felt nothing remotely like exaltation. This mysterious landscape, excessively literal in the sense that it was excessively silent, seemed the complementary inverse of the other one, the reality behind him that he inhabited, the city of Moscow, but also the entire network of cities and places that started there and stretched out, straddling the seas. The world seemed flat, dead, and hollow like the empty sea he was staring at now. He took a few steps amid the scraggy vegetation, the ground beneath which looked as if an army of invisible organisms had digested it and turned it into a dark, nondescript powder. From time to time he discovered some trace of human activity, for example a length of wire, old balled up sheets of paper, or shards of glass. These things, as if admitting their impotence through their sparseness, were not enough to allude to the atmosphere or past, let's say, of a community; they did not convey oblivion or neglect, either: it was an elemental abandonment, the traces of a vanished community. (The line from Giannuzzi bears repeating here: "It seems that culture consists in the thorough tormenting of matter and pushing it through . . .") From his vantage point, Felix could see the undulations of the gradual slope that formed the depression, slow and endless like the foothills of a large but not particularly tall mountain.

A stone had stopped rolling at the most predictable obstacle, another stone, and Felix thought the two might spend centuries in those exact places, untouched despite periods of freezing weather, sun, and shadow. It might seem strange, but it was this simple idea of unchanging cycles that moved him in the end; struck once more by the spectacle and the solitude, it occurred to him that he was the first person to discover that theater of neglect. He thought that the world ended right where he was standing (and that whoever managed to cross that flattened and rambling terrain, surely after years of futile attempts, would be faced with even greater desolation). As evening fell, the scene's surface changed color, without abandoning its metallic tint. Although there was nothing unusual about any of it, everything Felix saw seemed unique, and this exceptional quality confirmed for him that he was the protagonist of a discovery. This was enough to convince him to keep the moment a secret; he had found a desert as vast as a continent, despite having stumbled upon unintentionally.

Back at the hotel, as he crossed the lobby—which was even gloomier at that late hour—Felix wondered if Masha had returned yet. He imagined her bent under the weight of her purchases, skirting the ice, making laborious progress and in danger of taking a wrong turn at every corner, as he supposed she often did, though never without managing to find, sometimes with great effort, the way back to her designated route. A thought frightened him: she could become a threat in all her innocence if, on one of those chance detours, she discovered the territory. In reality, he wanted to keep it a secret as compensation for the Hotel Salgado's mysteries, all the things it concealed and never revealed. And though he didn't know what use he could make of his lunar valley, it was enough for Felix that it was his private discovery, something that expanded, let's say, his meager interiority, which was, even according to him, sparse by nature and with increasingly few experiences to support it. For a foreigner, discovery is no more than an unlikely manifestation of justice—one that is obviously off-limits to locals. Having dedicated a good part of his life to traveling the world in the hope of escaping the mental province to which he'd thought himself condemned, Felix realized in Moscow that his idea of experience had changed, or that it had always been wrong, or else had simply evaporated at some point, and that so many of the things he took for experiences in the past now barely left a trace on his hardened sensibility, having been transformed into almost unrecognizable states devoid of any real interest, of which nothing but a formless memory remained, impossible to recover except as a vague reminiscence.

Every experience was first consolidated as confusion, then was gradually transformed into forgetting. He had lost the thread of continuity with the past: his memories were floating moments unable to come together as a sequence, shards of events provisionally recovered that served only as fragments. The place as a whole, including the origin of the things in it, was something that would remain unknown. This produced in Felix uncontrollable states of bitterness that made him cowardly and indecisive, and led him to further mistrust his unpredictable and complex sensibility. I have occasionally thought of Felix as a two-dimensional person without psychology, contradictions, or even subjectivity. The same could be said of

Masha. An imprecise being with the mutable consistency of a dense fog, whenever she appeared she fluctuated like an abstract figure, say, at the mercy of the always-unpredictable interaction among currents of wind.

It seemed to me that both had invented themselves from the crudest, most trivial materials possible, each hoping the other might see them as an equal in their shared meagerness, and that this might, at the same time, be a way of inhabiting their own existence. Let's imagine that at some point—as if out of the blue, or from the combination of two strange elements—Felix's consciousness emerges, on the one hand, and Masha's, on the other. Gradually, and with great effort, both consciousnesses gathered enough energy to draw additional material to themselves, mostly things accessible to them by chance, like objects found on the unswept streets: odds and ends, papers, damaged scraps of wood, pieces of plastic. (Felix probably witnessed the capacity for survival of these materials when he saw them in their decades-long slumber in the barren plots around the residential complex.) In this way, they amassed a nucleus that began to hold in heat, increasing their chances of attracting even bigger, stronger, more flexible objects: pieces of fabric, sticks, or boards; whole containers, glass. And so Felix and Masha began taking shape, like two self-made figurines unexpectedly confronted with their own lives and respective consciousnesses. In both cases, lives and consciousnesses that would never be such, because they were artificial beings and therefore lacked any sense of intimacy or subjectivity, among other things.

I began thinking about that old friend of mine, Felix, and he seemed unrecognizable beside the person he currently was; though the same could not be said of Masha, because I'd known nothing of her before, though through a kind of assimilation with Felix it seemed possible to assign her (or, rather, draw from her) a series of attributes. "What does a friendship become?" I wondered. Its original intensity, a result of our seeing each other daily, had broken down over time into the sequence of sporadic lines Felix would send me, until it took the shape of a displaced feeling, gradually faded, which relied on a composition of snippets to adopt a new form. At some point, then, it occurred to me that Felix and Masha were like spirits, I don't know what else to call them, artificial beings, characters so completely available they could be put together like makeshift dolls. It is revealing that, in the age of instantaneous communication—when an incessant stream of electronic messages can reach you without any outside intervention, not even your own; when you could send messages all day long without any effort beyond that of writing, and sometimes not even that—at a time when communication has become so direct, Felix would still turn to the old system of postcards or notes written on hotel stationery, sent through the postal service. Another thing, I thought, that relegated my friend to the world of indirect developments, of divided courses, of interventions and prologues.

And so, as a character from another world, who, moreover, reached me by way of exotic objects—as I said earlier, those postcards and the protocols that govern their writing and mailing, with their allusions to travel that concealed more than they revealed—Felix had all the attributes of a fabricated being; not, say, someone without a soul, but rather an individual without a fully developed will whose movements were dictated by reflex and partial outbursts, each of which fulfilled only its own mission, whatever that might be, but never managed to compose a whole, a complete personality. For example, I have the sense that there was nothing coincidental about the way Felix paused in front of the photograph decorating his room during one stay, that famous photo titled "The Marionettist's Hands." Standing in front of it, he first felt implicated, then exposed, observed, and warned. The strings dangling from what was ostensibly a frame (a wall, the false back of a tableau, the suspended backdrop of an open-air theater, the balustrade around a rooftop) and indistinguishable from their own shadows, those strings were in fact directed at him, the invisible form on which the performance hung. Hidden in the immensity of Moscow, invaded by the cold and the darkness, Felix took another step back, reducing his fragmentary personality, and felt a sense of reconciliation; years later he found himself understood in his limitations, as if those tangled strings were still consoling him, saying, "Don't worry—be less, withdraw, we're here; to the right, now, and up . . ." As for Masha, she was increasingly a mere extension of Felix. If she'd had any aspiration to an autonomous life, as if she were real, it had vanished that first cold, dreary night spent condemned to wait for the being that justified her existence.

After his discovery, Felix tried to go about life as normal, or at least in a way that was similar to the life he'd had since arriving at the hotel. He sensed that something had changed, though he couldn't identify what it was. His impressions were so vague as to be essentially useless; he observed, for example, that the part of the city where he was staying seemed more desolate than usual. In his room, after performing the semi-acrobatic operations required to look out the windows, he surveyed the erratic angles of the streets, the large sheds or barns attached to the houses, the stairs out back, the internal patios and storehouses in general; that idyll of the countryside inserted into the suburbs seemed to him not only melancholy, as it always had, but also condemned to an incomplete life of eternal survival. His view was partial, but, having glimpsed and even wandered around it many times during his aimless walks, he could easily imagine the network of passageways woven outdoors between the sides and backs of the houses, which, over time, had been hidden in the unseen parts of the buildings. It was precisely this image of a clandestine village, the hidden face of the city, that led him to think that in Moscow things were subject to a contradictory form of time, at once accelerated and permanent. Before his discovery, though it had been common to see just a few people in the street, there had at least been, some facsimile of life and contradiction; now, however, when no one stepped outside, Felix thought they had all succumbed to the unique temporality of the city, that they had allowed the geography to swallow them.

Some afternoons offered no sign of life at all, others stood out for a lone sled gliding furtively down the street, as if animals were fleeing from something in terror. And so the city seemed to him like a complete world—without fissures, but fictitious—that revealed how it functioned, a plot that was visible at first glance in the different elements organized according to their roles and places in the hierarchy, that is, and also the practical uselessness of this organization. The streets, exaggeratedly straight and empty, clearly belonged to the order of the evident, but they also belonged to the order of the artificial, like the grid of a board game waiting for the pieces to be laid out. Moscow's "disuse," an emptiness Felix viewed as spontaneous, seemed to him to be the consequence of forgetting certain words. In this case, "people," or the less extreme "individuals." These things were no longer seen, as if from one moment to the next both word and idea had been eradicated from thought.

As for me, my thoughts turned to the world. To its increasingly powerful mechanisms and how we are inescapably destined to obey the working of its gears. These thoughts could only lead to the most pessimistic state of mind, into which I sank as if it were the sole respite or salvation permitted by an inevitable but still unrealized tragedy. And if I thought about the past, about the chain of events both shown and concealed, half-known or distorted, that is, about the series of actions that gave us the so-called "world today," though one way or the other it was an invented sequence, everything got much worse, because in the perpetual end of the road that is the present, unrelenting madness and eternal cruelty emerged as proof of humanity's wild ambition. Faced with such a somber and irremediable panorama, I thought, the only alternative would be to trust in artificial beings. I didn't expect them to provide some kind of justice or correct any wrongdoings, I simply imagined them as an alternative, a way of announcing that another world, also incomplete, would have been possible, and that this other world—insofar as it presented itself as a corrective to the so-called real one, or as its complement and commentary—was infinitely more fair.

The half-buried toy Felix saw at the residential complex, for example. Even with its marks of neglect and decay, so difficult to imagine for those who haven't seen them, that plastic figurine—heavy and solid like everything Russian—was, though mangled, the only complete being. It occurred to me that people were hobbled from the outset: a decisive emptiness fettered each and every mortal, and that this had become a human characteristic; in contrast, artificial beings—figurines made in factories, like the mangled one, or invented in the privacy of home when the most unlikely materials, forgotten and immune to sleep or dreams, come together on their own at night—represent everything people have not managed to be in the world as it stands. Given this, it was not surprising that the residential complex should be empty and lifeless; everything seemed meant to underscore the presence of the survivor, whose missing arm was perhaps the price he paid for his dealings with mortals. For his part, Felix held the figurine's presence up alongside the precarious or clandestine lives of the persecuted, who at the end of their lives are also the most forgotten: the poor migrant, the ostracized, the segregated.

One more among the displaced masses coming from those distant republics in a constant state of poverty, the figurine had appeared in Moscow's street markets behind a crate of fruits and tomatoes that he covered with a tarp to guard against the cold. If someone expressed interest he would pull back the cover, then lay it out again when they left. At the end of the day he would carry the crate and the rickety table it sat on back up to the top floor of a house he shared with several families; the artisans had set up their workshops in the stables, and there was farming equipment stored up in the attic. He walked between these instruments with care, afraid to touch anything, as if doing so would mean waking them and stripping them of the memory preserved by their stillness.

The figurine goes about his work as if it were permanent; he does not consider the possibility of change, nor does he even think that at some point his merchandise will run out and he should find a way to replace it. He does not understand how commerce works; to him, it is a surrogate for farming or, even more so, for gathering. Despite the distance, the loneliness, the different language, and even his nostalgia, the city seems like an extension of his village, so much so that he anxiously awaits the moments he can make his phone call, as if the remove became real only in that instant and vanished again as soon as he stopped talking. On the appointed days, the figurine stands in the long line outside the vestibule where they've set up the public phones. A cursory glance tells him that a few of his colleagues from the market are doing the same: he sees someone who seems to be from Mongolia, a Manchurian, and a Yupik man. When he thinks about these phone calls, he tells himself he is going to talk to "them," without specifying anyone in particular. That "them" means something, though, because when he thinks about the city of Moscow, about the multifaceted urban world that surrounds him and about most tangible manifestation of this new lifestyle, that is, the people, he uses the same word: "them." Felix imagines him with his hands in his pants pockets and his typical pensive demeanor as he goes over the things he still has to do that day. At some point, though, he will lose his arm; unlike the paper and cardboard artisans, miniature carpenters, or tinsmiths, the figurine will be able to adapt to his new condition and keep doing his job. The only difference is that, from now on, he will carry only the crate up to the attic at the end of the day, leaving the rickety table in the street, right where it was.

Felix tries to compare this image—of an uprooted individual with leathery skin and baggy clothes staring at the ground with his hands in his pockets—with that other image of the same person, in a similar posture and dressed the same way, but missing one arm, and the contrast is difficult to accept. In response to the greeting of some acquaintance, or to a confusing occurrence with no real explanation, the figurine must have felt the urge to lift his hand. But his first impulse was directed at his missing arm, producing a brief hesitation that unsettled whoever was waiting for his reply, and causing that person to interpret the fact as the typical delayed reaction of an immigrant. It was strange to see how the absence of his arm caught everyone's attention, but was then considered only in practical terms. It couldn't really be called suffering, either. No one thought of the figurine as an incomplete being, but rather as someone who had achieved his own version of wholeness. Meanwhile, the Moskva flowed slowly, partly due to the cold, and the figurine walked to one bridge or another to observe the water and the calm navigation of the blue steam that stretched across it. There, he gave in to simple thoughts; for example, it seemed like a miracle that the current was passing under him, that it was so slow and so quiet, and that he was in that exact place at that exact moment.

Felix dedicated several afternoons to making sure the limit territory was still where he left it. He went there in secret; the best way to do that, he thought, was to delay his approach. He made extraordinary detours on each trip, as if to avoid reaching the area near the linked buildings head on; every time he got close, as soon as he saw them stretching out to the sides like an endless gray snake, he felt a twitch at the base of his skull, which was his sign of apprehension: he was afraid the territory wouldn't be there anymore. Logically, though, he always found it, as desolate and somber as the antechamber to the under-world. Its depth, together with its unbelievable expanse, which presented no obstacle across its mineral surface, produced an unbroken sound like that of the void, a ravenous but quiet suction. If he looked back, the line of buildings rose up like a front line of frail, aimless ghosts turned into something mistakenly ornamental, a border no one cared to cross. Sometimes, when he walked toward them, aiming right up their center, he sensed that they were waiting in silence for him to draw near so they could close in and crumble down on him until the end of time. (Though this threat might never have been realized, Felix believed in things like that: the unexpected never happens, until it does.)

He paused before the immensity, feeling an ownership over it; he observed the vast emptiness and the distant, ambiguous light on the horizon for a few moments, thinking of nothing, until he retraced his steps with a strange sense of satisfaction, as if he had just renewed a peculiar sort of title. He left the place at nightfall, when he could make out the lights of the city, which had already been lit for a while. Crossing its wide avenues was an episode from which he emerged with tired eyes; the intense glint of the bulbs (in streetlights, headlights, the spotlights illuminating signs) on the accumulated ice blinded him. Masha vanished from his mind for days on end, except when he remembered her with apprehension, as someone capable of discovering the secret of that frontier. It was absolutely normal for Masha to disappear from people's thoughts, just as her own mind drifted, while she completed her chores, to her sole desire of closing herself in her cold room at the end of the day, counting the money, and imagining the book.

They both had their secrets, and in each the mysterious presence that secret represented, given the zeal with which they kept
it hidden, imposed itself as a new nature that distorted their
identities. Felix occasionally stumbled upon Masha's image, her
available external form: he'd watch her turn at the end of a hall
or walk past without seeing him. The same thing happened to
Masha: for example, from a dark corner of the lobby where no
gaze could reach her, she would watch Felix walk nervously
beside the reception desk with his splintered personality, afraid
someone might discover the truth about his comings and goings.
When he returned to the hotel after his walks, Felix sometimes
felt he was stepping into a temple dedicated to a defunct cult, or
a palace devastated by neglect. It wasn't just that the building's
permanent shadows were discordant with the diaphanous light
of the city, but rather that despite the age of the walls and the
irreparable wear and tear to the objects between them—from
functional devices to ornaments, including several instruments
fallen out of use, all of which were immediately visible, like
the aforementioned sheets of hotel stationery piled in every
room, or the worn or broken soap dishes in the bathrooms—
despite all this accumulated age, the hotel constantly revealed
its makeshift nature. And so one imagined that some terrible
and sudden event had taken place and everything had been preserved exactly as it was in that moment.

Things were different in Masha's book. There, she was
a woman of means who—giving in to family tradition and
the despondent apathy that tends to afflict millionaires, and
also respecting a promise reluctantly made to her father on his

deathbed—grudgingly ran a hotel that, in any event, required minimal effort to maintain. She did little in her free time, though she would never have admitted it was free time, that is, a series of sequential moments at her complete disposal to fill as she pleased. She spent it at a few of the building's unusual windows, which, from their different heights and placement in the most unlikely corners, offered completely contradictory views of Moscow, as if it were a city made of snippets, or rather a city built to be viewed only partially. It was impossible to see it as a panorama, and this was the result, thought Masha, of the fact that the city had been constructed, and later rebuilt, in successive stages of concealment; its aim was not to house, let's say, the suffering or vulnerable population, but rather to avoid the gaze of the Hotel Salgado. As such, from the countless windows Masha found at her disposal, she could examine a truer, more partial, and more compressed city, like the individual pieces of a puzzle. Moscow resembled a scale model or, rather, several of them united by a strange bond of solidarity that connected them only insofar as it foregrounded their differences. Masha would get lost as soon as she set foot on the pavement (in this, she was no different from the real Masha) and the incomplete, deformed views that she remembered taking in from the hotel were now transformed into menacing and often grotesque apparitions on the verge of collapsing onto her, multiplied by the continuity of streets and the strange orientation of the houses and buildings.

Felix enters the hotel one night, long after Masha has shut herself in her room; with the natural but reticent air she will come to know well, he asks if they have any rooms available. The hotel is, in fact, practically empty, so Masha arbitrarily picks a direction. She walks with her eyes closed, confident in her extended arms and in her knowledge of the building's layout and quirks, which are etched into her memory down to their smallest detail. One of the times she pauses to wait for Felix to recover from a start provoked by the thick darkness and the unknown, or simply to catch up to her in the shadows, she registers his approach as freezing air on the back of her neck. In the book, Masha reflects on this man's mysterious presence, who extends his stay over and over for no apparent reason. A free and apparently uncomplicated person, she thinks, who nonetheless dedicates himself to enclosed spaces and the convoluted streets of the city.

A few pages later, she intermittently hears the nocturnal sounds of Felix's slumber through the walls: he seems to be advancing and retreating. The inaudible murmur and spontaneous, incomprehensible words rely on the silence in order to become something else; a shout occasionally dissolves into a series of inarticulate noises. Sometimes she recognizes his presence in the empty city she moves through on her way to the market like a wedge cutting through the glacial air. Felix's presence only appears coincidental at first glance: Masha notices the care he puts into going unnoticed. It is nearly impossible to hide in a deserted city. The whole place seems distant, muted, and foreign, but since it is the only one she knows, she is prepared to admit that she would probably feel the same way in any other city; she views everything with detachment, finds cause for disgust and incomprehension on every corner, and sees in the wide avenues framed in gray a pitiful melancholy that displays their outdated beauty like a mediated form of decay. This urban landscape remains immutable; she has never seen any change in it: the streets and facades begin each new season of snow in the exact same condition in which they bid farewell to the last, just a few weeks earlier. This fact is not simply boring; it unfurls as a coiling, condensed, tormented monotony.

At this point in her plot, Masha understands that Felix must be derived from her. For some unknown reason, she had begun to gather, let's say, heat and an array of substances and materials; she accumulated these with distracted patience until, grown and relatively autonomous, they formed the nucleus of what would later take the shape of Felix. Though Masha thinks this is a figurative way of understanding things, and Felix would certainly agree, the form it takes as a symbol is so true that it alters nothing essential. In a different time, Masha's reaction might have been to withdraw, fall into a deeper silence than usual, and lose herself in one of the routine managerial activities so often mentioned in the book; on this occasion, however, she has an unexpected reaction, which consists of freeing herself from the fiction constructed between them and, as such, impose on her guest a relationship of dominance. She will dominate him through the hotel, the only place in Moscow where Felix has found refuge, but which nonetheless will insistently set obstacles in his path.

Once Felix, struck by the hotel's silence and above all by the image of Masha, which took shape and quickly vanished again like a ghost, is alone in his room he sits on the nearest bed to think. He has been wandering around for hours and is exhausted. Of his arrival in the city he remembers the cold train station, the wide stairs and high ceilings, and the pastry stand he found when he stepped into the street. Nothing after that, except for the vague impression of having crossed inhospitable avenues and an endless chain of interconnected plazas. He assumes that an unknown force guided him to the Hotel Salgado. What was he looking for? Where had he come from? In Masha's book, Felix is unable to answer these questions, which further illustrates his diminished condition; not as a person completely devoid of free will or consciousness for any profound or circumstantial reason, but rather as someone who, obeying some strange force, has chosen to hide and not act, or to act only partially, according to his diurnal or lunar mood.

Between the cold walls of the room packed with useless beds, without any sign of windows or the outside world, he cannot imagine what floor of the building he is on at the moment, immersed as he is in the constant cavernous thrum, like a mill set to pulverize the building's foundations. And so, newly arrived, he finds himself at the mercy of his dismay. He opens his only suitcase, spreads his few articles of clothing out across one of the beds, and lays down on another with such contained desperation that the creak of the wood sounds to him like a cry of fear, or warning, that hangs in the night air until he falls asleep.

Meanwhile, Masha couldn't care less that the plot of her book includes elements taken from reality. Felix, the hotel, the city, even those old walls and building's quirky structure, to say nothing of herself, are simply entities able to step out of the book without any significant consequences for their true condition. Nonetheless, she can't explain why she prefers the consistency she finds in its pages, even if all that would still exist and the sun would continue to shine on the Moskva if the book were to disappear. Everyday life, the concatenation of events that typically occur all around her, and even the more or less unexpected ones that reality sometimes delivers, seems predictable to Masha, and therefore not stimulating enough to be read. Even so, there are no guarantees about the imagination that draws on this world, and the imagination that tries to oppose or deny it might be even more insignificant. Masha understands, then, that she is faced with at least one unresolvable dilemma: she does not believe in books or characters, but she herself is little more than faded substances grouped together by chance and unceremoniously set in motion. Come to think of it, she realizes that she has never read a book before, a fact she does not regret, given the scant and lackluster lessons her book has to offer. As such, she does not see the principal use she has found for it as strange: just as she was made wealthier by the currency she discovered in the wardrobe, she assumes that the book is also enriched when its pages are used to store money.

Back then, in that other time, when we were young and held our heads high, we had no idea what lay in store for us. Like the old Sicilian said, whoever makes the mistake of leaving can't make the mistake of going back. It's an assertion that, as far as I know, Felix has never repeated, most likely because the idea of returning never crossed his mind. The day he left, I stayed there on the quay; the truth is, from the moment he stepped aboard the boat and they began to ready the port and blow horns that probably meant many different things, events moved too quickly for anyone to notice my presence near the docks. Later, as everyone began to leave on foot or by car and not a single person paid me any attention, I wondered if Felix's absence had made me invisible. Something similar occurs in puppet shows, when for one reason or another a character disappears in the eyes of the others, but of course not from his perspective, or for the audience that unquestionably gives him life, though not enough.

In any case, silence and withdrawal took over as soon as the ship began to recede; the dock went back to being a point that was forgotten, constructed, and forgotten again on some unspecified sector of the map. Just like Felix's thoughts about being last or, rather, his feeling or belief that he was last, that day I also felt I was the last person in that theater of sadness and despair. As I said before, I was the first one at the port as the night came to an end. I watched Felix arrive early, and found it strange that such a corporeal being—with all his luggage, besides—was about to embark on a long absence, the duration of which could not be clearly defined. Then we went on our walk along the quay with the warehouses, a brief stroll punctuated by stops and half-dialogues. Later, I was a witness to the ceremonies of leave-taking and, lastly, stared at the river and watched the boat fade into the imprecise strip that was the horizon, as in so many scenes from paintings and films.

I have, however, a more detailed memory of the afternoon and evening that followed, during which I was absorbed for hours, lulled into drowsiness perhaps by the profound and unbroken silence, watching the birds (pigeons and sparrows) search greedily for food with their eyes so close to the ground they seemed nearsighted. That silence, those minor facts of life that could be revoked at any moment, since nothing seemed more likely than those few birds deciding to take their search somewhere else in the port or the city, indicated to me that something was about to end; night would fall and as it did, this part of the world would emigrate to the dark side of the moon, perhaps never to return to the light, and I would remain, for anyone who might later by interested in the area by the piers, as the only witness to that final evening. Night fell suddenly, despite the languid sunset, though not before the birds started taking refuge in the few surrounding trees, their song producing isolated murmurs that underscored the silence and gave the impression that in each tree a secret or a confession was being drawn out.

This evening song lulled me to sleep. I remember sitting on a granite bench as cold as a gravestone, and turning my eyes to the water. The sun was slipping behind the broad continent and at my back was the immense strip of land separating the city from the mountains; consequently, the river's surface, which was already normally quite still, looked like an oily carpet, its slow swirling forming just a few whitecaps across its surface. And so I nodded off, I don't know whether from boredom or exhaustion, staring at the water as if it were a marshy lunar landscape. When I awoke, it was already night; my sleep had made the twilight pass surprisingly fast. In contrast to the morning, when odors spread out fresh and distinct, not yet macerated by the heat of the day, what surrounded me now was air saturated with silt and humidities, proof of the unbearable temperature and intense weariness emanating from the earth at that hour. If I turned and looked up, I could see a distant, cloudy bell of illumination above a series of small geometric figures composed by lights organized into diagrams; these were buildings in the city. If I looked straight ahead, I could see the depths of a dark night.

A few points of light appeared in the distance, some of them intermittent, probably a motorboat or steamer moving through the thick darkness. I imagined that the boat taking Felix probably looked like that, too, a metal crust surrounded by that immense liquid mass, leaving its trail of vacillating light, always on the verge of disappearing into the blackness. As the night went on, those buoyant lights grew scarcer, and I suppose there was a moment just before dawn when they vanished entirely. By then, the noise from the city had also faded, the ground had cooled, and the water's lapping sounded both clear and insubstantial, as patient as the constant erosion of beaches, cliffs, quays, and piers. And so the night continued its work without obstacles or distractions, the swift navigation of astral bodies seemed like a leisurely stroll, a haven of stillness before the noises and glints of the day took over. At a certain point, from the leaves of a plane tree off to my side, I thought I heard a muffled, or stifled, shriek. I looked over at the tree and caught a glimpse of a slight rustling in the leaves that couldn't have been produced by the breeze and that somehow expressed the same thing, that is, a stifled movement. I thought about two animals fighting, or birds that were either nocturnal or lost in their nightmares. But that wasn't the strangest part: just then, as I was trying to determine the source of a cricket's sporadic intervention, I saw a majestic cylinder of light stretch from the river straight into the sky.

I don't know if it makes sense to go into detail, though I should say that no one would have been able to explain this phenomenon. The column of light remained visible for a long time, and to this day I wonder if it's still there, appearing regularly in the middle of the night, and whether I stopped seeing it back then not because it went out, but rather because it was hidden by the morning light. The dew and the humidity had wet all the surfaces nearby: the bench and gravel and stone paths around me, along with the rugged terrain flecked with fledgling vegetation and the sparse surrounding trees. I was soaked, as well, thought I didn't notice this until I lifted my hand from the bench and saw its opaque, dry silhouette.

My religious experiences had always been tied to more or less human activities (rituals, venerations, offerings, and so on); this was the first time one resulted from a natural event, or something that at least seemed not to involve human intervention, though I wouldn't go so far as to say it was supernatural, and it gave me a feeling of fear and vacillation, of admiration, and also of shock. The wide column of light wasn't close by, but I would also be hard pressed to say it was far away; in any case, its unusual brilliance, which seemed to impose itself on its surroundings with calm but imperturbable force, probably due to the absolute darkness of the night, eradicated distance and became the only protagonist capable of carrying that moment. I had a fleeting memory of those distinctive scenes in science fiction: a protagonist from another time or a visitor from outer space descends to Earth inside a glowing tube that gradually dissipates (this is the end of the journey) to reveal the pallid, dazed being that just successfully completed the process of transubstantiation. Its body has traveled in the form of light for days and days to cover the extraordinary distance, leaving behind a fading metallic sheen as evidence of its passing. In contrast, the column was lit up for a long time and clearly exerted a force of attraction on everything around it. Despite the distance, my exhaustion, and how my eyes burned when I looked directly at it, I couldn't look away; the solitude and shadows around me seemed empty and unimportant beside that extraordinary, if sadly uniform, spectacle.

So anyway, I also saw that what I had taken for small clouds of volatile substances or steam related to the column of light or the difference in temperature, was in fact a legion of small organisms or insects apparently attracted to the unexpected light, which were launching themselves at it, resolute and orderly, as evidenced by the way they swirled around it, testing the power that had brought them together in that place and would somehow, I thought, mark the end of the lives they had known. Below the surface of the water, the decimated river fauna was probably also congregating. Then I had another absurd thought: I thought that the strange nocturnal dust was hurling itself into the column of light in order to make an interstellar journey. (Tiny intelligent beings swarming on the surface of the water near the shore, always ready for any opportunity to travel and colonize another world.) But the course that was charted—whether blind, intentional, or desperate—meant a sacrifice even if it didn't ultimately end a life. Who could guarantee they would still be the same people when they reached their destination? Science fiction also expressed doubts about this (to say nothing about the unlikeliness of making the return trip). As such, I did not feel I was in a position to venture a truth about what I was observing, much less while in the presence, because of the night, of the stars and the strange phenomena produced, and of the wild course the planet was charting through outer space.

I wondered only whether, given exemplary height it reached, holding its shape along its entire length and not allowing even a single particle of energy to filter off sideways, I wondered only whether the column of light had caught anyone else's attention, given that people in the city must certainly have been able to see it. It was such a treacherous phenomenon that it might, like so many things that were evident, suddenly become invisible. I could not come up with an answer, and since then have not been able to find an explanation, though I have tried to do so countless times; all I know is that I was afraid of being the only audience to that scene. It was not a fear of any danger or punishment I might face as the result of some supposed intrusion, but rather the idea that the condition might imply assuming some special responsibility, a duty or a mandate, even if it were simply to keep quiet. (I now see how similar this experience was to how Felix felt about the limit territory: his fear of being discovered, or of being accused and ultimately unmasked.) Meanwhile, I thought that night at the port, Felix was crossing the silent, calm sea. To this day, I still don't know whether the column of light gradually went out or whether it was hidden by the prologue to the onslaught of morning. I do know that it started getting weaker just before the day really made its presence felt, until I could see a kind of sovereign decision or a voluntary defection on the part of the light, which opted to die before being completely overwhelmed by the sun's rays.

When all this was over and the morning had definitively begun, I prepared to abandon the granite bench and retrace the many steps between the port and my house. As a farewell, I looked at the plane tree off to the side, from which several of the birds from the day before had already begun to come and go; it occurred to me that the image would make a good idyllic memory of that morning. When I tried to stand up, though, some force prevented me. I don't know whether it was the sleepless night, the loneliness, or the nocturnal phenomena I had witnessed, but the fact is that I found myself at the mercy of a complete and total disorientation. I had no idea where I was, or to which order of reality the landscape surrounding me in that moment obeyed. Even the idea of myself contained a fundamental contradiction, as I believed myself to be at once the invisible stranger observing me and the real person who had set out on a journey toward forgetting. And so I awoke as if out of a dream, as if Felix's departure had occurred in a distant and almost immemorial past that manifested through intermittent ideas or recollections. Then, as I will explain in greater detail, I left the area by the port and returned to the city proper along the same route I had taken on the way, and also thinking the same thoughts.

It was well known that Moscow, perhaps as a result of urban planning, ends abruptly. Felix was fascinated by this. It is possible to locate a point on the map, or the grain of dust or wisp of vegetation on the terrain, that sits outside the limits, which makes it possible to say, "here is the city, everything past here is not." In this way, every interested observer unintentionally reproduces the gesture, though of course not the impulse, of the squatter, of the settler, of anyone who establishes a border to define what is internal and what is external. As a result, anyone right at the outskirts of Moscow would get the sensation of sinking into the depths of territorial desolation. The forces in play were the same ones unleashed in the continent's distant epicenter, and the consolation of being near the city—in case something went wrong and someone, say, urgently needed an overcoat—quickly evaporated because everyone immediately felt transported to some immense expanse in the distance. Seen from the air, the city looked like an old fortress frozen in time; the world around it had reshaped itself, erasing all trace of past urban influences on the surrounding areas and reaching the city limits as if it were a military assault or a flood's slow embrace. The highways oriented in all different directions reinforced this feeling of isolation and loneliness: in their emptiness and silence they were like lines drawn on a vast, nameless map. It seemed contradictory to Felix that things were so scarce, so meager in a way, in that land of formidable distances, and that they were also so marked and defined. He looked up at the sky and saw three birds industriously flapping their wings as they flew in a straight line; in that exact moment, they crossed the city limit and were lost in the direction of the steppe.

Masha's book tended to associate Felix with these kinds of meanderings, almost always related to observation, which assigned him the role of reflecting on more or less vague occurrences, usually something having to do with the adjacent landscape or some apparently spontaneous event. Her intuition had proven itself yet again by immediately noting the true nature of the person—in this case, Felix—and determining the best way to dominate him, so that his undefined personality, always open to the next distraction, would bend readily to her will. For example, there comes a time when she tires of imagining Felix's nationality; his name, easily confused or forgotten, has a dubious ring to it in Russian, like Salgado's. Felix could come from anywhere, which is why Masha needs to dispel the uncertainty; it is a detail that will help her compose his profile, which has been shrinking rather than expanding over the course of his stay. It might be mere coincidence, but when she asks the question (she tries to use a semi-bureaucratic phrase that her custom of dealing with the public has imposed on her, though this same habit has also worn the phrase out, leaving it entirely meaningless) Felix seems to go transparent, as if his upper body were dissolving into the air.

They are facing one another in the lobby; it is night, and Masha remembers the late hour and similar silence when Felix arrived. And just as he was back then, he is still enveloped in the cloud of nocturnal mist that has followed him in from the street and performs strange operations on his body, breaking it apart or making it evaporate, Masha can't say exactly, but in any event, endowing it with a dose of transparency, a few slight but decisive gradients, as if his flesh and his clothing had conspired to make themselves less dense. This effect will imbue the scene with a sense of mystery, but by unspoken agreement it remains hidden; Felix does not know what to say (he may not even be aware of what is going on) and Masha is unable to think (the speed at which these events unfold unsettles her). It is disturbing to watch his form darken and go translucent as if it had turned into a screen, especially the area around his shoulders, right near the edge of his body, where his clothes hang by their own weight from his skin, and his neck. This is how Masha sees through Felix: not by discerning how things really are, but by looking at them as if through a dark and granulated window able only to offer glimpses of smudged masses with difficult contours. She completes the vague images of Felix's shoulders and neck, then, with her detailed knowledge of the Salgado's lobby: the lighter patch in the back that is a window, and the dense, vertical plane of the door.

When she heard Felix say "Argentina," that he was of Argentinean extraction, Masha was not inclined to believe him; she thought he had just invented the country and for some reason was hiding the truth from her. But my friend insisted so forcefully, tapping his fingers on the reception desk, that Masha resigned herself to acting as though she found the information credible. In any case, it would be perfect for her book: there was nothing better for a fake protagonist than an invented nationality. Masha knew she could direct or mold Felix as much as she pleased, just like the little polar bear on her nightstand and the countless objects, made of every material imaginable, that children in Moscow use as toys. Felix did not particularly mind that she didn't believe him, either; even he sometimes doubted his origins, that is, he questioned the existence of his country as a homeland or region. He knew he had a national affiliation similar to a civil document, that is, a passport, but he found the meaning and concrete effect this might have on his character increasingly mysterious. And yet, as the importance of his own origin disintegrated, the world's other countries and regions—with their wide range of sub-nations, autonomous territories, mini-countries, and super-states—began to seem more decisive. He trusted in nationalities as if each one were a cell in a tray for sprouting the seeds of idiosyncrasies and unique attributes; only Argentina's was an orphan identity, an empty slot with inhabitants who belong to a separate world, before history, class divisions, and the existence of languages or religions. This is why Masha's distrust was, for Felix, a gesture of recognition, a nod to his neutral and undefinable condition. No one asked him anything, or made a single comment, as if he didn't exist, as if he were invisible, or were the last member of a dying tribe.

On one occasion, as the evening drew to a close and he sat waiting in his room for the depths of night, by some spontaneous association Felix remembered the figurine from the residential complex and imagined it as a being whose nationality was absent, scattered, or dissolved by the passage of time, stemming perhaps from an era before its own existence, always waiting for some unlikely astral alignment, maybe just to have something to wait for, that might reestablish its forgotten nature at some point in the past. The world plunges into its blind and autonomous wandering all the time, he often said to himself, so it makes sense that there would be bands of individuals getting temporarily and then definitively lost. The figurine must belong to one of those waves, and Felix thought that, had it not been for his slight dimensions, he might have taken it for a real person. Inert as it was, like a rock, it still seemed that day like the most eloquent object he could have found in that place. He had bent over to get a closer look, and was surprised to find that the surface around it conformed to the figurine's scale; the visual field matched its dimensions, rendering it bigger and more convincing. The surrounding area guaranteed the creature's existence, like a hidden garden or primal environment. It was just a few centimeters from his shoe and wasn't even half as long, but Felix was still able to assign it dimensions that could, at any moment, become human if the gaze falling upon them accepted the illusion.

Given that Masha's book should be, at least in part, about men who change nature, it did not seem off the mark that in other respects (physiognomy, physical proportions) the figurine would resemble the peoples of distant republics, who always arrived in the city at the same time of year, like permanent fixtures on the calendar, after digging canals, draining swamps, and making endless roads that in principle went nowhere. They came on vacation, or sometimes without a future after relinquishing their strength or some part of their body, and were received at first like heroes for their labors, until the memory began to fade just as the year ran out and the next batch of workers was about to arrive.

This made Felix think that the figurine could be one of the masses thronging the cold streets illuminated by snow; not as a person like any other, given that it was obviously a fabricated being, but instead as an imitation, the facsimile of a person that, as such, asserted—perhaps even beyond its own desire and the intentions of its creators—the existence of a passive, displaced life. It didn't matter that this existence was also hidden, the essential part was that it be somewhat visible. Felix questions the meaning of life, since it is a thing so easy to represent. (Those figurines, which probably outnumber living beings, including all the different species and types of organisms, assert with their silence that life could be like them.) He imagines himself as part of a community of people made from plastic, wood, or any number of other materials; being the only living member of the group, he enjoys, let's say, an obvious mandate. This all begins on the first of the year, when everyone is still a bit disoriented and unsure of the ground they tread on; as happens in animal fables, there is no way to have the figurines express themselves except by means of human ideas and phrases. Felix realizes this right away and, in his optimism, assigns the figurines names and qualities related to their morphology. They say complexity is unlikely in recently formed communities, so he reverts to a superficial system of classification. For example, he calls the figurine made of wood "the hard worker," while "the strong one" is made of iron (or another metal), and the one made of cloth is "the soft one." The most enigmatic moniker goes to the figurine made of plastic, who becomes "the artificial one."

Felix tries to make life in the community as real as possible, but by the fifteenth of January he already understands that the only true thing about it is the illusion of cohabitation, which is so close to fiction and for which he is almost entirely responsible. He imagines his room in the Hotel Salgado, where the figurines also sleep, having assumed the role of travelers passing through. In this he finds a justification for the extra beds, and he is surprised by the agility with which some of them can clamber up to the sill of the higher window. Sometimes he is awakened in the middle of the night by the footsteps of someone headed down the hallway to use the telephone, trusting that the time difference will mean their relatives will already be up. This makes Felix think about objects in general, like the telephone, or the beds, and how their artificiality—insofar as they are man-made objects and therefore subject to invention, first, and then fabrication—has more in common with the hyperartificial condition of figurines than it does with humanity. They are beings that know nothing of delirium or nightmares;

through their silence, because they only express themselves if Felix arranges it, they reveal a trace of life that eludes life itself. This vestige is reminiscence: even if none of them has existed in reality, there is a real model behind each one, thinks Felix, that could appear at any moment but remains latent in the meantime, waiting for some human confluence to wake it. This is the fascinating thing about dolls, he thinks during a night of insomnia, there is no trickery or complex operation; they always seem ready to take on life and movement.

And so, during that sleepless night, he remembers a photography exhibition. Felix has arrived at an old, dilapidated home with high walls that smells of stale air, dust, and moisture, as if the restoration, or demolition, had been interrupted by the end of the workday. It has been night for several hours and through the silence he hears his own breath as a sustained sigh of resignation. He had been walking all afternoon, he'd breathed the sickly air downtown in that city facing the ocean, and eventually found that mansion from another time with its simple poster, lit by a single spotlight in the dark night, announcing a documentary exhibition about the era of political violence.

As he walks from one room to the next, he gets the unhappy sensation of visiting misery. What is being exhibited is something at once familiar to him and unknown; both things, what he knows and what he does not, overwhelm him. He has a general base of information that is not entirely useless, but still is not sufficient to help him fill in the images. The result is weariness and detachment, as well as a feeling of having betrayed the intentions of the exhibit and, to a certain extent, the memory or lesson it wants to communicate. He had seen few people on the street before entering, and not a single car during his entire walk along the avenue that skirts the coast. The city seemed empty, as if a disaster had occurred but left no trace; as he walked, it occurred to Felix that he seemed to be playing one of those eccentric individuals who remains completely unaware they are in the middle of a catastrophe. Perhaps due to this, and to the stillness he encounters in each room, he thinks he is the only visitor (and the last, as always). He also assumes that the exhibition's guards are still conversing quietly among the shadows outside the entrance, having chosen the breeze off the water over the atmosphere indoors, as they were when he arrived, the darkness under the trees obscuring the embroidery and ornamentation of their uniforms, which, vaguely evoking a policeman's, are meant to make them seem more important than they are.

Felix thinks about the images hanging on the walls, about what they are meant to represent, and remarks to himself that he never felt so confused anywhere else. A gentle breeze filters in through the cracks in the dilapidated walls and rustles the photographs like a ghost; it is in this moment that he is startled to notice that someone has materialized at his side: a woman with Asian features stares at the photo in front of her, unmoved. Her body is covered by a single article of clothing, a long raincoat that skims the ground. Felix runs his eyes across the floor and sees something like a surface of dirt mixed with or concealed by little pieces of different things, probably remnants of the residence's masonry or its old flooring, and realizes this was the reason he hadn't heard her approach. They exchange a surprised or apologetic smile, which my friend can't sustain because when he turns back to the photographs he sees two corpses tossed haphazardly onto a farm wagon.

As if it were a recent but hazy memory, he understands now that those bodies did not seem real to him at first: he took them for extravagant or outrageous subjects that silently changed temperature and, as they grew increasingly solid, dedicated themselves to achieving a stiffness similar to a human's. He'd always thought that dolls should telegraph their condition as fabrications in order to be believable; now it seemed to him that those two bodies had managed to resemble their models by revealing their artificiality. Felix imagines two short, imprecise characters walking through the high altitude desert toward the farm wagon, obeying an imperious order they had not been able to resist, which was that they die—the greatest proof of its authority was this photo in which they appear, rigid: the photo of a deed done. Doubt insinuates itself only in their postures. Accustomed to seeing corpses in restful poses or funereal solemnity, whoever sees these bodies might wonder about their unnatural appearance. Indeed, Felix thinks that their poses seem forced, as if death found them in that exact place and they got stuck imitating dead weight—denied, let's say, even posthumous physical relief. Meanwhile, the involuntary desire for a next breath is etched onto their faces like a living expression.

One of the victims has almond-shaped eyes, like the woman in the raincoat. Felix tries to see the man's face in more detail, but the glint of the sun shining directly on it makes this impossible. It seems risky to turn around just then, he is afraid the woman will sense his thoughts; as a consolation, he recalls the image of one of the guards, who also had Asian features, responding to his greeting from the shadows as Felix entered the building. He isn't sure whether to believe in the coincidence, rather, between the late hour and the dilapidated residence, he is not entirely sure where he is.

In some of the rooms there are banners or placards on the walls: these are commentaries, explanations, or timelines. Perhaps without meaning to, they recall the tapestries and curtains that probably adorned the residence's main rooms in its heyday, when it was the home and above all the quotidian space of a wealthy traditional family. (This, Felix now realizes, is another thing that old estate overlooking the sea has in common with the Hotel Salgado and its past as a distinguished mansion that constantly made its presence felt, despite erstwhile frequent maintenance and extensions.) Extending the comparison, the photos exhibited that day would be the paintings from before, stripped of their ornamental frames and their aristocratic motifs. He has read in several advertisements, and also on the large and small posters he sees everywhere he goes, that the exhibition seeks to illustrate the political violence that descended on the country and lasted for decades, an experience that has not been fully processed and which tends to be erased from collective memory, though it remains as a trauma or as an unknown, or as both things at once, for much of the population. Felix thinks that this task, like so many others, is an impossible one: it would require an infinite archive disseminated without pause. He finds it unsettling that something as old as violence could have this new element, that is, being the object of observation and study; as if everyone needed to know they came from the era of the crime, from that sordid aspect of history, in order to understand some part of themselves for the first time, whether as victims, or not.

Intentionally or otherwise, the images have an ambiguous effect. Some are brutally direct in the way they present the violence but, to Felix, these are dulled by their exhibition. The path through the show, the way it is divided thematically, the entire home filled with photographs, even the recorded voices of a few of its protagonists, characters who were deliberately murdered hours after saying something that is now repeated day and night in certain rooms like an eternal nightmare or a message from beyond the grave; the idea of offering violence up for contemplation or presenting it as a series of curated documents seems to Felix like a means of enduring it. On one hand, the aftermath is not part of the photos, its manifestation was more drastic; as such, the exhibition is a way of showing what happened, as if the images were trying to recover the events from the cloud of ignorance into which they had settled, to endow them with the presence they once had. On the other hand, the photos are stable images: they waited, there was time to select them and, later, to hang them on the walls, where now they wait for visitors' eyes to fall on them. Felix takes short, cautious steps through the space, as if he were in a museum, the same way he supposes everyone else does.

Sitting in his room, which happens to look a lot like the galleries in the exhibition, Felix remembers identifying two groups or types of photos. One showed events in progress, while the other showed the effects of what had happened; the distinction was hard to establish and at times could seem arbitrary or unnecessary. Some of the images, for example, consisted of razed plots of land and inert bodies, the general aftermath of destruction followed by neglect; others showed the episode as it was happening (ceremonies, requisitions, protests, confrontations, and so on). The photos in the first group were scenes of death or desolation, and Felix imagined the reactions of the other people who went to see the show (they probably tried to look away, sometimes without success). He was moved, however, not by the cruelty that these beings endured, but rather by the isolation and loneliness of the category that had been assigned to them: individuals from a bygone era, now under observation. (Not by denying their displacement and the autonomy, say, they'd achieved at the end of their lives, but rather through the crime, centered on their bodies and emphasized as an example, which perhaps inadvertently made them occupy an problematic space between redemption and scorn.) In contrast, the photos from the other group showed living subjects for the most part; Felix thought these seemed especially theatrical, performances designed to confirm the spontaneous apathy inspired by the dead, whose images appeared just a few meters away in every room. They were scenes that reflected another time. Felix found it paradoxical that the photos of corpses could still have such force, as if the bodies occupied a perpetual present and never stopped being models of death, while the images of the living, with their clothes, postures, and backdrops providing definitive marks of their vintage, were the ones that seemed to age.

Between all the doors, vestibules, antechambers, corridors, and the path indicated by red cardboard arrows hanging from the walls, the house unfolded like a labyrinth the visitor was meant to improvise a way through. As such, Felix was not surprised to find a new grand hall, two hours into his visit. He thought again how dances and social events must have been held there, in its heyday. Now, though, the walls revealed years of neglect through cracks, holes, and various layers of peeling paint. The ceiling, with its array of mutilated, unrecognizable ornaments, seemed more menacing because it was so high. That this room had retained its importance was evident in the fact that they had hung just two large photos on the side walls, which Felix imagined had been covered with mirrors in the old days. The photo on the left was of the short and narrow main street in a small town that could not accommodate all the people who had gathered there. It was hard to tell where the picture had been taken from, it was neither a particularly low angle nor a high one, and Felix imagines the photographer climbing up an electrical post. There are no women or children in the image, but it seems like the whole town is gathered. This might be due to the people's faces, which—all looking in the same direction

172

or intensely focused, absorbed in their thoughts as if trying to remember a script and waiting for whatever might happen next, things that give off an air of importance—give the sense of a neighborhood assembly.

Each group (residents, protesters, policemen, dogs) is identifiable by its particular clothing or uniform (or, in the case of the dogs, by a complete lack of clothing) and because each acts as one might expect under the circumstances. There are also police vans and regular unmarked cars, and a line of small businesses on either side of the street, each one with its small or eye-catching sign. The political conflict is supposed to present itself in this world, which seems built for a different purpose and dedicated to other things. Despite the lack of space produced by the cars, each group has found its place. The protesters occupy one half of the block and are looking toward the police, who have taken the other half. Then there are the other residents, the onlookers, and the dogs, who watch both groups indiscriminately with their backs to the storefronts, though their gaze does seem attentive and in some cases quite specific. Given the content of some of the other photos, Felix finds this scene quaint and somehow innocent; however, he thinks there are—or, rather, he thinks he sees—strings extending upward from each individual, strings that most likely govern the actions of these beings and where they turn their eyes.

Now, in the Hotel Salgado, he remembers this fact and realizes it did not catch his attention then, though he certainly found it difficult to understand. Felix imagined the townspeople convened in a narrow mountain valley as if it were a point isolated somewhere in the depths, visible only through a combination of chance and the world's indifference. The strings left the photo and spread along the walls, mingling with the fissures and cracks, or maybe they sketched them, making themselves look like delicate, disguised trails of shadow stretched toward the ceiling, as if the individual townspeople had agreed to offer an alternate version of themselves: less willful and perhaps more fatalistic. This had nothing to do with ideology or political conflict, Felix thought, but rather with people's need to ensure their survival, even if not everyone was aware in that moment what was happening to them (this fact might be clearest in the case of the dogs). Felix believes that in this locale, in the midst of this solitude and due to an unusual combination of circumstances, the hidden ability to temporarily reduce one's being and present oneself according to an alternate nature revealed itself in the brief moment the photo was taken; people so overwhelmed by their considerable or meager free will that they need to rest, to delegate, to become someone or something else.

Felix feels he is in the uncomfortable position of needing to decipher the obvious. The photo on the opposite wall shows another scene: a desert with stony summits in the distance and lower peaks in front of them. The white line of a highway can occasionally be seen, crossing and dividing the mountains, as if their upper reaches belonged to an alternate, inaccessible world. Subtle variations in light and color, shadow and depth, create a series of interconnected visual planes that, thinks Felix, exist in perpetual conflict. Despite the sharp angles of the terrain, with its daunting precipices, ledges, and ravines that in some cases look impassable, the view is presented from a distance under the friendly rubric of an orderly landscape. A few places on the peaks are hidden from sight, and it is possible to imagine something like rural strongholds there, tiny fields resembling yards or vegetable gardens. There is no trace of animal life.

In that house built a few meters from the ocean, Felix sees the images of those people left naked and dead, each in a different pose, numb and rigid, occupying the imposing wall assigned to them. The bodies are scattered according to no apparent logic, but they have all been tossed from a vehicle driving in a straight line, its wheels leaving two pale strips of earth behind them. This produces the contradictory sensation of disarray and deliberateness, as if a new layer of ordered forms had added itself to the silence. The third or fourth figure is a half-buried man in a strange, almost vertical, position with his head and one arm raised, like a swimmer mid-stroke. Neutral elements that might go unnoticed but are still relevant surround this scene: the uniform gray of the sky, the desert landscape described above, the irregular peaks and vast stretches of rocky terrain. Of all the bodies—the opaque nakedness of their skin contrasting the pallor of the rocks; the thick mounds of hair between their legs, under their arms, and on their heads like appliqués made of wool or cloth stuck there to make their presence more vivid—the half-buried man is the most enigmatic and the only one that inspires, through his action, a sense of life. Nonetheless, this extravagant activity makes him less believable; Felix thinks that he has chosen simulation, which is what separates him from fabricated beings.

Perhaps this is due to the artificiality of his position, which one tends to associate with acting. Beyond what the photo's description says, he thinks, this excessive detail renders the whole scene somewhat theatrical, and this theatricality is practically the only trace of human behavior.

Alone in the middle of the room, Felix passes an aesthetic judgment (then immediately feels ashamed and looks around to see if anyone has noticed): he finds the victim's pose exaggerated, almost like an impersonation; it does not represent the cruelty inflicted on him or his pain at the end, but only the repetition of a gesture. He is also unsure why there is something like a smile on the man's face. One might fall back, he thinks, on the old cliché that death found him at peace, with a clean conscience and no outstanding debts; that even though he wasn't looking for it, it brought him the satisfaction of an obligation fulfilled anonymously and, as they say, to the fullest. In his room in the Hotel Salgado, he thinks if he could see that photo for the first time (strangely, he says "See it again for the first time"), perhaps the memory of the figurine would be different, maybe it would change as a result of that experience. Felix went on thinking things like this as he lay sleepless throughout that long winter night.

Well, as people sometimes say as they take their leave, I think it's time to gather my things. Up to this point, I have described a few of Felix's dubious adventures and the related commentaries that came to my mind several years ago, after receiving his simple note from the Hotel Salgado. I remember opening the envelope with a pair of heavy scissors, feeling the paper's resistance and hearing the crunch that brought me right back to my childhood, when I would cut card stock or cardboard in school. Inside the envelope was the small sheet of paper, folded in two; the paper was as rough and thick as parchment and had dried out from the passage of time, turning the fold into a cleft that threatened to break it in two. In any case, the writing occupied the top half, while the only thing on the lower half was the signature—a clarification that was unnecessary for me and would be illegible to anyone else. His signature was like a private ideogram I never bothered to understand or decipher. I knew it was his, and that was enough. Moreover, for someone who didn't know Felix, or didn't know that particular scribble was his and somehow represented him, the person behind those words didn't matter. (He was writing, which presumably meant something, but from a place of non-existence.) As time went by, the little sheet of paper eventually tore and, as if this were the beginning of some legend, the message and signature were separated forever due to my chaotic lifestyle and disorganized relocations. The message ended up in my yellow folder and Felix's signature was simply lost. I didn't take the precaution of taping or attaching the pieces some other way when I had the chance; the consequence being that one day, when I saw the text by itself for the first time, I took it as proof that we (me, him, everyone) were gradually fading into oblivion.

Only a few years had passed since then, but the difference between the lines written in his hand and the others, the truly anonymous ones he had copied in his hotel room, was almost entirely effaced; I even thought that, in some fair or even-handed way, the words had returned to their original lack of definition, as if it were a stronghold they defended with all their strength, even in times like these, forging alliances with objects from the material world in order to preserve their indeterminate nature. Without a signature, the letter was incomplete—and this was entirely in keeping with Felix's elusive personality.

One last memory from the morning he left from the port of Buenos Aires: as preparations began to accelerate, a series of alarms or horns sounded on board, inviting the travelers' companions to disembark. I had chosen to stay on land along with several others, most of whom were elderly or physically impaired. A little while later, the companions began to emerge and I noticed how some of them, having said goodbye to the real travelers just a moment before with a hug on the deck, simulated an arrival as they descended the gangplank. They were children and youths returning to the autumnal land of old age, where a group of elderly people awaited them with little idea of what to do with them, eyeing them with a mix of incredulity and incomprehension, the way they tended to look back on their own youth. The joke distorted what should have been reality.

Earlier, while, as I said, Felix and I talked in front of some warehouses with our eyes fixed on the cobblestones, I told him about a thought I'd had that morning. I'd been walking from the neighborhood of Retiro out to the docks. Past the old Torre de los Ingleses, I noticed the glint of the streetlights reflecting off the paving stones, which seemed to move on their own due to the undulations of the road. The trucks drove slowly at that solitary hour and I thought to myself that the day would soon unfold, bit by bit. Once I'd passed the market or street fair that was there back then, and which might still be, I began to see the pale shadows of a few major buildings from Perón's time—the Hospital Ferroviario and a few others, all imposing and austere—which grew clearer as I approached. And I had an idea or, rather, a desire: inexplicably, it occurred to me to knock down everything that had been built, alone and outfitted with a single hammer—a task to which I would apply myself over days of solitary but efficient labor. Today, I see this as one of those things that is said for the sake of speaking, or to avoid mentioning something else. Nonetheless, Felix's reaction was surprisingly practical. After thinking for a few moments, and with his eyes still glued to the ground, he said that one hammer wouldn't be enough: one way or another, it would break or end up unusable before the job was done, due to the wear and tear.

This notion of reality, as if words should be carried to their ultimate consequence, intrigued me. I had never thought of it that way. It was a convincing argument, but I found it hard to believe that, if treated with care and in a hypothetical situation, a hammer might not be able to do all that was asked of it, no matter how arduous the task. Now I understand: the truth is that I never planned to finish the job, or probably even start it. Instead, I saw it as a slow and secret labor, repeated over several days without making any progress. Come to think of it, this stasis was what I wanted for my own life—not inaction, but rather the absence of change, and also a task that would justify my existence to others, whatever opinions my personal choices might generate. Maybe Felix was searching for the same thing, along a different path. His choice proved to be the most correct and the one best suited to the way things move; whereas I was not able to avoid the snares of immobility.

Sometimes I think there is a puppeteer directing my steps and those of everyone we know, Felix included. Our awareness is always partial; moreover, we seek to conceal and to show ourselves at the same time. The next morning, once the column of light had faded and the day had definitively begun, I passed the same places near the port and in Retiro on my return as I had on my way there. My clothes were soaked, as I said, and I was feeling slightly drugged from exhaustion. Felix's goodbye, the preparations aboard the boat, and the start of his extended journey that still continues today—all that seemed to occupy a distant moment. I would not be exaggerating if I said that those things seem closer to me now than they did then. A new era began that morning, a new time: one of waiting for the next memory to emerge.

SERGIO CHEJFEC, originally from Argentina, has published numerous works of fiction, poetry, and essays. Among his grants and prizes, he has received fellowships from the Civitella Ranieri Foundation in 2007 and the John Simon Guggenheim Foundation in 2000. He currently teaches in the Creative Writing in Spanish Program at NYU. His novels, *The Planets* (a finalist for the 2013 Best Translated Book Award in fiction), *The Dark*, and *My Two Worlds*, are also available from Open Letter in English translation.

Heather Cleary's translations include Roque Larraquy's *Comemadre*, which was longlisted for the National Book Award for Translated Literature, César Rendueles's *Sociophobia*, Sergio Chejfec's *The Planets* and *The Dark*, and a selection of Oliverio Girondo's poetry for New Directions.

OPEN LETTER

WWW.OPENLETTERBOOKS.ORG

Elsa Morante (Italy)
Aracoeli
Giulio Mozzi (Italy)
This Is the Garden
Andrés Neuman (Spain)
The Things We Don't Do
Jóanes Nielsen (Faroe Islands)
The Brahmadells
Madame Nielsen (Denmark)
The Endless Summer
Henrik Nordbrandt (Denmark)
When We Leave Each Other
Asta Olivia Nordenhof (Denmark)
The Easiness and the Loneliness
Wojciech Nowicki (Poland)
Salki
Bragi Ólafsson (Iceland)
The Ambassador
Narrator
The Pets
Kristín Ómarsdóttir (Iceland)
Children in Reindeer Woods
Sigrún Pálsdóttir (Iceland)
History. A Mess.
Diego Trelles Paz (ed.) (World)
The Future Is Not Ours
Ilja Leonard Pfeijffer (Netherlands)
Rupert: A Confession
Jerzy Pilch (Poland)
The Mighty Angel
My First Suicide
A Thousand Peaceful Cities
Rein Raud (Estonia)
The Brother
João Reis (Portugal)
The Translator's Bride
Mercè Rodoreda (Catalonia)
Camellia Street
Death in Spring
The Selected Stories of Mercè Rodoreda
War, So Much War
Milen Ruskov (Bulgaria)
Thrown into Nature
Guillermo Saccomanno (Argentina)
77
Gesell Dome
Juan José Saer (Argentina)
The Clouds
La Grande

The One Before
Scars
The Sixty-Five Years of Washington
Olga Sedakova (Russia)
In Praise of Poetry
Mikhail Shishkin (Russia)
Maidenhair
Sölvi Björn Sigurðsson (Iceland)
The Last Days of My Mother
Maria José Silveira (Brazil)
*Her Mother's Mother's Mother and
Her Daughters*
Andrzej Sosnowski (Poland)
Lodgings
Albena Stambolova (Bulgaria)
Everything Happens as It Does
Benjamin Stein (Germany)
The Canvas
Georgi Tenev (Bulgaria)
Party Headquarters
Dubravka Ugresic (Europe)
American Fictionary
Europe in Sepia
Fox
Karaoke Culture
Nobody's Home
Ludvík Vaculík (Czech Republic)
The Guinea Pigs
Jorge Volpi (Mexico)
Season of Ash
Antoine Volodine (France)
Bardo or Not Bardo
*Post-Exoticism in Ten Lessons,
Lesson Eleven*
Radiant Terminus
Eliot Weinberger (ed.) (World)
Elsewhere
Ingrid Winterbach (South Africa)
The Book of Happenstance
The Elusive Moth
To Hell with Cronjé
Ror Wolf (Germany)
Two or Three Years Later
Words Without Borders (ed.) (World)
The Wall in My Head
Xiao Hong (China)
Ma Bo'le's Second Life
Alejandro Zambra (Chile)
The Private Lives of Trees